Kidnapped by a vicious race of Lizard Men from Fire Island, the young men of Oyster Bay face a grim future of slavery, starvation and lingering death. Their master here is the mad and dangerous Lizard King, who holds sway over his land of mutants by the eerie powers of black magic and voodoo. YOU are the only one who can hope to rescue the suffering prisoners, but do you have the courage to risk this dangerous mission?

IAN LIVINGSTONE is an internationally known figure in the Fantasy Games world. He is one of the founders of Games Workshop Ltd. in England, the largest U.K. company specializing in fantasy games. Mr. Livingstone lives in England.

ALSO AVAILABLE IN LAUREL-LEAF BOOKS:

Ian Livingstone

ISLAND OF THE LIZARD KING

Illustrated by Alan Langford

LAUREL-LEAF BOOKS bring together under a single imprint outstanding works of fiction and nonfiction particularly suitable for young adult readers, both in and out of the classroom. Charles F. Reasoner, Professor Emeritus of Children's Literature and Reading, New York University, is consultant to this series.

Published by
Dell Publishing Co., Inc.
1 Dag Hammarskjold Plaza
New York, New York 10017

This work was first published in Great Britain by Penguin Books Ltd.

Copyright © 1984 by Ian Livingstone

Illustrations copyright © 1984 by Alan Langford

Laurel-Leaf Library® TM 766734, Dell Publishing Co., Inc.

ISBN: 0-440-94027-3

RL: 6.7
Printed in the United States of America

First U.S.A. printing—January 1985

For Roy Coleman

CONTENTS

ISLAND OF THE LIZARD KING

HOW TO FIGHT THE CREATURES
OF FIRE ISLAND

Before embarking on your adventure, you must first determine your own strengths and weaknesses. You have in your possession a sword and a backpack containing provisions (food and drink) for the trip. You have been preparing for your quest by training yourself in swordplay and exercising vigorously to build up your stamina.

To see how effective your preparations have been, you must use the dice to determine your initial SKILL and STAMINA scores. On pages 18–19 there is an *Adventure Sheet* which you may use to record the details of an adventure. On it you will find boxes for recording your SKILL and STAMINA scores.

You are advised to either record your scores on the *Adventure Sheet* in pencil, or make photocopies of the page to use in future adventures.

Skill, Stamina and Luck

Roll one die. Add 6 to this number and enter this total in the SKILL box on the *Adventure Sheet*.

Roll both dice. Add 12 to the number rolled and enter this total in the STAMINA box.

There is also a LUCK box. Roll one die, add 6 to this number and enter this total in the LUCK box.

For reasons that will be explained below, SKILL, STAMINA and LUCK scores change constantly during an adventure. You must keep an accurate record of these scores and for this reason you are advised either to write small in the boxes or to keep an eraser handy. But never rub out your *Initial* scores. Although you may be awarded additional SKILL, STAMINA and LUCK points, these totals may never exceed your *Initial* scores.

Your SKILL score reflects your swordsmanship and general fighting expertise; the higher the better. Your STAMINA score reflects your general constitution, your will to survive, your determination and overall fitness; the higher your STAMINA score, the longer you will be able to survive. Your LUCK score indicates how naturally lucky a person you are. Luck – and magic – are facts of life in the fantasy kingdom you are about to explore.

Battles

You will often come across pages in the book which instruct you to fight a creature of some sort. An option to flee may be given, but if not – or if you choose to attack the creature anyway – you must resolve the battle as described below.

First record the creature's SKILL and STAMINA scores in the first vacant Monster Encounter Box on your *Adventure Sheet*. The scores for each creature are given in the book each time you have an encounter.

The sequence of combat is then:

1. Roll both dice once for the creature. Add its SKILL score. This total is the creature's Attack Strength.
2. Roll both dice once for yourself. Add the number rolled to your current SKILL score. This total is your Attack Strength.
3. If your Attack Strength is higher than that of the creature, you have wounded it. Proceed to step 4. If the creature's Attack Strength is higher than yours, it has wounded you. Proceed to step 5. If both Attack Strength totals are the same, you have avoided each other's blows – start the next Attack Round from step 1 above.
4. You have wounded the creature, so subtract 2 points from its STAMINA score. You may use your LUCK here to do additional damage (see over).
5. The creature has wounded you, so subtract 2 points from your own STAMINA score. Again you may use LUCK at this stage (see over).
6. Make the appropriate adjustments to either the creature's or your own STAMINA scores (and your LUCK score if you used LUCK – see over).
7. Begin the next Attack Round by returning to your current SKILL score and repeating steps 1–6. This sequence continues until the STAMINA score of either you or the creature you are fighting has been reduced to zero (death).

Escaping

On some pages you may be given the option of running away from a battle should things be going badly for you. However, if you do run away, the creature automatically gets in one wound on you (subtract 2 STAMINA points) as you flee. Such is the price of cowardice. Note that you may use LUCK on this wound in the normal way (see below). You may only *Escape* if that option is specifically given to you on the page.

Fighting More Than One Creature

If you come across more than one creature in a particular encounter, the instructions on that page will tell you how to handle the battle. Sometimes you will treat them as a single monster; sometimes you will fight each one in turn.

Luck

At various times during your adventure, either in battles or when you come across situations in which you could either be lucky or unlucky (details of these are given on the pages themselves), you may call on your LUCK to make the outcome more favourable. But beware! Using LUCK is a risky business and if you are *un*lucky, the results could be disastrous.

The procedure for using your LUCK is as follows: roll two dice. If the number rolled is equal to or less than your current LUCK score, you have been lucky and the result will go in your favour. If the number rolled is higher than your current LUCK score, you have been unlucky and you will be penalized.

This procedure is known as *Testing your Luck*. Each time you *Test your Luck*, you must subtract one point from your current LUCK score. Thus you will soon realize that the more you rely on your LUCK, the more risky this will become.

Using Luck in Battles

On certain pages of the book you will be told to *Test your Luck* and will be told the consequences of your being lucky or unlucky. However, in battles, you always have the option of using your LUCK either to inflict a more serious wound on a creature you have just wounded, or to minimize the effects of a wound the creature had just inflicted on you.

If you have just wounded the creature, you may *Test your Luck* as described above. If you are Lucky, you have inflicted a severe wound and may subtract an extra 2 points from the creature's STAMINA score. However, if you are Unlucky, the wound was a mere graze and you must restore 1 point to the creature's STAMINA (i.e. instead of scoring the normal 2 points of damage, you have now scored only 1).

If the creature has just wounded you, you may *Test your Luck* to try to minimize the wound. If you are Lucky, you have managed to avoid the full damage of the blow. Restore 1 point of STAMINA (i.e. instead of doing 2 points of damage it has done only 1). If you are Unlucky, you have taken a more serious blow. Subtract 1 extra STAMINA point.

Remember that you must subtract 1 point from your LUCK score each time you *Test your Luck*.

Restoring Skill, Stamina and Luck

Skill

Your SKILL score will not change much during your adventure. Occasionally, a page may give instructions to increase or decrease your SKILL score. A Magic Weapon may increase your SKILL, but remember that only one weapon can be used at a time! You cannot claim 2 SKILL bonuses for carrying two Magic Swords. Your SKILL score can never exceed its *Initial* value. Drinking the Potion of Skill (see later) will restore your SKILL to its *Initial* level at any time.

Stamina and Provisions

Your STAMINA score will change a lot during your adventure as you fight monsters and undertake arduous tasks. As you near your goal, your STAMINA level may be dangerously low and battles may be particularly risky, so be careful!

Your backpack contains enough Provisions for ten meals. You may rest and eat at any time except when engaged in a Battle. Eating a meal restores 4

STAMINA points. When you eat a meal, add 4 points to your STAMINA score and deduct 1 point from your Provisions. A separate Provisions Remaining box is provided on the *Adventure Sheet* for recording details of Provisions. Remember that you have a long way to go, so use your Provisions wisely!

Remember also that your STAMINA score may never exceed its *Initial* value. Drinking the Potion of Strength (see later) will restore your STAMINA to its *Initial* level at any time.

Luck

Additions to your LUCK score are awarded through the adventure when you have been particularly lucky. Details are given on the pages of this book. Remember that, as with SKILL and STAMINA, your LUCK score may never exceed its *Initial* value. Drinking the Potion of Fortune (see later) will restore your LUCK to its *Initial* level at any time, and increase your *Initial* LUCK by 1 point.

EQUIPMENT AND POTIONS

You will start your adventure with a bare minimum of equipment, but you may find or buy other items during your travels. You are armed with a sword and are dressed in leather armour. You have a backpack to hold your Provisions and any treasures you may come across.

In addition, you may take one bottle of a magic potion which will aid you on your quest. You may choose to take a bottle of any of the following:

A Potion of Skill – restores SKILL points
A Potion of Strength – restores STAMINA points
A Potion of Fortune – restores LUCK points and adds 1 to *Initial* LUCK

These potions may be taken at any time during your adventure (except when engaged in a Battle). Taking a measure of potion will restore SKILL, STAMINA or LUCK scores to their *Initial* level (and the Potion of Fortune will add 1 point to your *Initial* LUCK score before LUCK is restored).

Each bottle of potion contains enough for *one* measure, i.e. the characteristic may be restored once during an adventure. Make a note on your *Adventure Sheet* when you have used up a potion.

Remember also that you may only choose *one* of the three potions to take on your trip, so choose wisely!

HINTS ON PLAY

There is one true way through to the Lizard King and it will take you several attempts to find it. Make notes and draw a map as you explore – this map will be invaluable in future adventures and enable you to progress rapidly through to unexplored sections.

Not all areas contain treasure; some merely contain traps and creatures which you will no doubt fall foul of. You may make wrong turnings during your quest and while you may indeed progress through to your ultimate destination, it is by no means certain that you will find what you are searching for.

It will be realized that entries make no sense if read in numerical order. It is essential that you read only the entries you are instructed to read. Reading other entries will only cause confusion and may lessen the excitement during play.

The one true way involves a minimum of risk and any player, no matter how weak on initial dice rolls, should be able to get through fairly easily.

May the luck of the gods go with you on the adventure ahead!

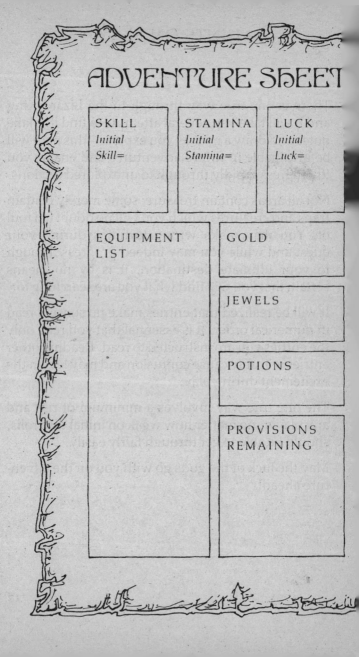

ADVENTURE SHEET

SKILL	STAMINA	LUCK
Initial	*Initial*	*Initial*
Skill=	*Stamina=*	*Luck=*

EQUIPMENT LIST

GOLD

JEWELS

POTIONS

PROVISIONS REMAINING

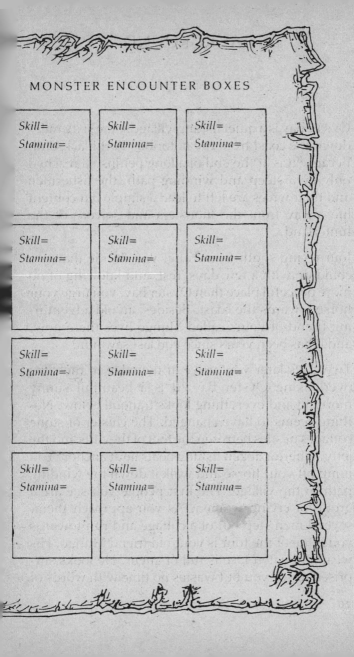

MONSTER ENCOUNTER BOXES

Skill= *Stamina=*	*Skill=* *Stamina=*	*Skill=* *Stamina=*
Skill= *Stamina=*	*Skill=* *Stamina=*	*Skill=* *Stamina=*
Skill= *Stamina=*	*Skill=* *Stamina=*	*Skill=* *Stamina=*
Skill= *Stamina=*	*Skill=* *Stamina=*	*Skill=* *Stamina=*

BACKGROUND

Oyster Bay is a quiet fishing-village some sixty miles down the coast from the notorious Port Blacksand. Because it is at the end of a long peninsula reached only by a steep and winding path, the fishermen and their wives are left to lead a simple but content life, away from the monsters and sorcery of the hinterland.

Journeying south from Fang, you decide that you could do with a few days' rest, and knowing of no more peaceful place than Oyster Bay, you urge your horse towards the coast. Besides, an old adventuring friend of yours called Mungo lives there now, and it has been years since you last saw him.

Two days later you arrive at the edge of the cliffs overlooking Oyster Bay. It is a beautiful sunny morning and everything looks tranquil below. Nothing seems to have changed. The cluster of stone cottages nestles between the foot of the cliffs and the jetty, where a dozen fishing boats lie at anchor. You jump off your horse and walk it down the winding path to the village. The first people you see are a group of crying women. As you approach them, several men step out of a cottage and run towards you. One of the four is your old friend Mungo. His weather-beaten face is full of anger. He looks surprised to see you but wastes no time with words of welcome. He recounts the sad events that have befallen the village.

Having no gold or material wealth, the people of Oyster Bay thought themselves safe from raiders attacking their village. But several weeks ago, while most of the men were out at sea, the Lizard Men of Fire Island landed their boats in Oyster Bay and kidnapped several young men. Mungo believes that they are now enslaved on Fire Island and working in chain gangs in the gold mines. Since the kidnapping, two men were left to guard the village while the rest went out to fish. Despite this, the Lizard Men attacked again this very morning, overpowering the guards and taking away more young men. Mungo tells you that he is about to set sail for Fire Island alone because the other fishermen are too scared to set foot on the island. He stares at you in silence until you smile and say that you will aid him in his quest. He slaps you on the back and shakes your hand in gratitude. For the moment the poor fishing folk forget their grief and crowd round you, eager to thank you. Mungo then invites you to dine with him and rest awhile, as the voyage to Fire Island will take several hours. Over a delicious feast of boiled lobster and salad, you discuss your plans.

Mungo tells you that he does not think that humans live on Fire Island any longer, but his knowledge is fairly limited. These are just rumours that pass between fishermen from other coastal villages; however, it is known that Fire Island used to be a prison colony, guarded by a tribe of paid Lizard

Men. This was a rather futile attempt by Prince Olaf to rid his land of undesirable characters. The good prince soon learned that it would have been simpler to put his lawful citizens on Fire Island and leave the evil-doers on the mainland; there were just too many of them. He gave up his attempt and abandoned the prison colony. When the Lizard Men received no pay, they took their vengeance out on the prisoners and the island became a place of terror ruled by a Lizard Man prison-guard who proclaimed himself King. The prisoners were forced to dig mines in the hope of finding gold for the Lizard King. They were underfed and ill-treated and many died; that is presumably why the Lizard King is sending out his men to find new slaves. It is known that in order to assert his authority, the Lizard King began practising voodoo and black magic. He also started genetic experiments in an attempt to breed an invincible race of Lizard Men. Most of the experiments went wrong. Grotesque mutants were created, and some of the harmful potions found their way into the water drains, with terrible consequences. The local flora and fauna were affected, with the result that man-eating plants developed and giant beasts evolved. A few of the prisoners managed to escape the island on rafts and were picked up by fishermen, but what has happened in the last few years, nobody knows. Fire Island had almost been forgotten until the recent raids. Success in your quest to assassinate the Lizard King and rescue the kidnapped victims is doubtful, but you must try.

You stand up and walk down to the jetty with Mungo, stepping aboard his small fishing boat. In the sight of cheering villagers, you untie the boat and push out to sea, wondering if you will ever return.

NOW TURN OVER

Mungo's years with the fishermen of Oyster Bay have made him a skilful boatman. He swiftly hoists the sail of the small boat and sets a course due west across the silvery-blue sea. The land soon recedes into the distance, and you sit back on the deck, relaxing in the afternoon sunshine. From the stern you hear merry whistling, the creak of the rudder, and Mungo occasionally calling out to a seabird passing overhead. You think about the good times you used to have with Mungo, his constant cheerful nature and willingness to help people in need. You find it difficult to believe that so much evil exists in the land when there live the likes of Mungo. As the hours drift by, you talk and laugh, trying to ignore the dangers ahead. Mungo is always one to tell a tale and he is now telling you about his father and how he used to work in a travelling circus. 'He was a big man, big as a mountain,' laughs Mungo, 'and he would do just about anything for a paying crowd. Wrestle Trolls, have elephants stand on him, and even let a Killer Bee sting him! He was a tough old customer, but he finally met his match in the north. The circus was in Fang as one of the attractions during the festivities surrounding the Trial of Champions, and my father decided on a whim to enter. He walked into Deathtrap Dungeon and, alas, was never seen again. He was really too old for such an ordeal, although there was no telling him that. But at least he tried.'

Just as Mungo is about to tell you his next tale, he jumps up and shouts 'Land ahoy!' at the top of his voice, as though he were yelling the news to the crew of a galleon. You look to where he is pointing and see Fire Island in the distance. The island sits on the sea like a green cushion, with a jagged mountain protruding from it. Smoke gently curls up from its top: a volcano's fuming anger waiting to explode.

Mungo steers the boat towards a small inlet at the eastern tip of the island, hoping that it will remain concealed between the high rocks. You both put on your backpacks and clamber out of the boat to begin your quest to find the Lizard King. If you wish to scramble round the rocks to the beach in the cove to your left, turn to 24. If you wish to clamber over the rocks on the other side of the inlet to the beach in the cove to your right, turn to 33.

2

The Shaman places three nutshells on the ground and explains that under one of them lies a bead and you have to choose the correct one. *Test your Luck*. If you are Lucky, turn to 358. If you are Unlucky, turn to 326.

3

The Dwarfs, suddenly encouraged by the possibility of freedom, turn to help you slay the guard with their hammers. The Lizard Man falls to the ground under a barrage of blows and the Dwarfs begin to cheer. They smash open their shackles and gather round to thank you and to quench their thirst with the water in the pail. You tell them of your quest to kill the Lizard King and they all offer to help. You ask them where the other prisoners are, and hear that they are working in other chambers deeper in the mine. You tell the Dwarfs to lead you there as quickly as possible (turn to **161**).

4

The tunnel gradually widens and your feeling of claustrophobia recedes. Before long you are back at a T-junction. If you wish to turn left, turn to **101**. If you wish to turn right, turn to **44**.

5

Thrusting your sword into the Rattlesnake's dark lair, you hear the dull clang of metal striking metal. You forget about the Rattlesnake and try to scrape the metal object out of the hole with your sword. In the sunlight you see a magnificent golden winged helmet. If you wish to place the helmet on your head, turn to **292**. If you would rather leave the helmet and walk carefully down into the gorge to head west, turn to **119**.

6

Drinking the liquid makes you feel dizzy, but your body feels charged with energy. Add 1 SKILL point and 2 STAMINA points for drinking water brought from an enchanted stream. Refreshed, you walk over to the door in the far wall (turn to 353).

7

Pressing on further west, you notice that the ground is becoming wetter and softer. Soon you are ankle-deep in water. The trees thin out and you find yourself wading through thick black mire. The marshland stretches out in front of you as far as you can see. Suddenly you hear the sound of squelching behind you and are surprised to see a strange creature run past you. It is small with green reptilian scales. Its arms are long and hang down to the ground, and it moves rapidly over the marsh on its webbed feet. It pays you no attention. If you wish to call out to the creature, turn to 317. If you prefer to keep trudging west, turn to 158.

8

You reach the corner and look down the corridor. It ends at a doorway, but a hunch tells you to climb the spiral staircase (turn to 82).

9

You whisk the iron bar out of your backpack and thrust it between the jaws of the vicious Crocodile. It is now helpless, with its jaws wedged open, and you are able to push your raft away from it (turn to 390).

10

It is so dark inside the bore-hole that you cannot even see your hand in front of your face. If you still wish to crawl down it, turn to 34. If you are having second thoughts, and would rather back out and carry on down the tunnel past the hand-cart, turn to 321.

11

The Dwarfs have dealt with the other Orc and turn to help you in your struggle. The Orc is soon defeated (turn to 121).

12

You struggle on through the dense jungle, and suddenly stumble over a human skeleton. The maggots and insects have long since devoured the flesh, but the clothing looks like that of a prisoner who must have tried to escape. You wonder how he or she died. There is a hand-axe and some rope lying by the prisoner which you decide to take before continuing north-west (turn to 105).

13

You do not see a TARANTULA crawling down the trunk of the banana tree in the semi-darkness. Your hand presses down on its plump, furry body, and before you realize what you have done, the spider has bitten you. Lose 3 STAMINA points. The shock makes you slip. Roll two dice. If the total is the same as or less than your SKILL score, turn to 381. If the total is higher than your SKILL score, turn to 118.

14

The river meanders gently through the low hills. As you sweep round the next bend, you see a group of mud huts close to the left bank. You steer the raft into the bank to avoid being seen by any of the huts' inhabitants. Jumping off, you creep forward through the trees to get a better view of the huts. Standing behind one of the huts, you see two tall reptilian creatures wearing armour and carrying whips and curved swords – LIZARD MEN! If you have read the message in the snuff-box, turn to **63**. If you have not read the message, turn to **270**.

15

Your constitution is strong enough to shrug off the disease, and your temperature soon returns to normal. You untie your raft and push your way up-river (turn to **379**).

16

You pull off your backpack and throw it down the log. You crawl quickly inside and lie perfectly still, bleeding and exhausted. Lose 1 STAMINA point. Moments later, you hear the Headhunters running by. *Test your Luck*. If you are Lucky, turn to **380**. If you are Unlucky, turn to **313**.

17

You walk back down the hill and turn left towards the volcano (turn to **303**).

18

The nuts and berries taste delicious. The Pygmies know what is good to eat in the jungle. Add 2 STAMINA points. Suddenly one of them utters a shrill cry and they all vanish into the undergrowth. You breathe a sigh of relief and begin again to hack your way west (turn to **7**).

19

This section of the tunnel looks as if it has been disused for a long time. The beams supporting the ceiling are cracked and look unsafe. You arrive at the edge of a vertical downward shaft, not far beyond which the tunnel ends. There is no ladder running down its side for you to descend. If you are wearing red leather boots, turn to **392**. If you have not found these boots, turn to **246**.

20

You crush the other egg with your boot before climbing up the volcano as you cannot walk across the sulphur pool (turn to **178**).

21

You sheathe your sword and walk over to the edge of the pool. If you still wish to drink the water, turn to **92**. If you would rather head off west again, turn to **222**.

22

The Lizard King is so terrified that he drops his fire sword. You leap forward and pick it up to attack the Lizard King with his own destructive weapon. Add 2 SKILL points. He can hardly overcome his fear to defend himself, but the Gonchong finally forces him to fight.

LIZARD KING   SKILL 10   STAMINA 15

If you win, turn to **153**.

23

You pick up the Lizard Man's pail, as it contains water which you imagine would be very welcome to the thirsty slaves. You walk on until the tunnel opens out into a chamber (turn to **223**).

24

It does not take you long to reach the beach, which is small and covered with golden sand. A few rocks jut into the sea, and at the far end of the beach you see a tiny hut made of white stone. The roof has collapsed and the hut looks deserted. There are some long tracks in the sand, criss-crossing the beach. If you wish to walk across the beach to the hut, turn to **211**. If you would rather climb back to the inlet and over to the beach in the other cove, turn to **33**.

25

Three more Grannits uncurl themselves and shoot forward to bite your legs. You manage to jump over them, but the first is still clinging to your shin by its teeth. You hack at it with your sword.

GRANNIT   SKILL 4   STAMINA 3

If you win, turn to **85**.

26

You open the pouch and look inside but cannot see anything; it is totally black inside. You decide to drop a stone into the bag to see what happens. The stone disappears from view and the pouch does not become any heavier. You have found a Pouch of Unlimited Contents. Add 1 LUCK point. The pouch will enable you to carry large and heavy objects simply by placing them inside. These objects are actually transported to another dimension and will weigh nothing inside the pouch, but can be retrieved at any time. If you have not done so already, you may:

Drink the liquid in the phial	Turn to **311**
Try on the boots	Turn to **94**
Put the ring on your finger	Turn to **297**

If you do not wish to carry out any of these actions, you may continue your way west again across the grassy plain (turn to **222**).

27

As the day wears on, the sun gradually sinks into the western horizon. It sits like a big red balloon on the sea next to the volcano before falling out of sight. The sunset shades of pink and purple radiate across the sky and soon the air is filled with the noisy sound of thousands of insects. You decide to camp down for the night between two bushes, hoping to remain hidden from any nocturnal predator. *Test your Luck*. If you are Lucky, turn to **388**. If you are Unlucky, turn to **348**.

28

Again the tunnel splits at a junction. If you wish to turn left, turn to **226**. If you wish to carry on straight ahead, turn to **101**.

29

As the Hydra closes in on you, you reach for your sword and prepare to fight.

	SKILL	STAMINA
HYDRA (left head)	9	9
HYDRA (right head)	9	9

Both heads will make a separate attack on you in each Attack Round, but you must choose which of the two you will fight each time. Attack your chosen head as in a normal battle. Against the other you will throw for your Attack Strength in the normal way, but you will not wound it if your Attack Strength is greater; you must just count this as though you have defended yourself against its bite. Of course, if its Attack Strength is greater, it will wound you. If you win, turn to **389**.

30

You are walking in a determined way towards the volcano, when a large creature springs out in front of you from behind a large rock. Its grotesque torso is covered with ugly warts and saliva drools down its long chin. You have been ambushed by a HILL TROLL.

HILL TROLL   SKILL 9   STAMINA 9

Unless you are wearing Sog's helmet, you will lose the first Attack Round. If you win, turn to **65**.

31

You pick up your pole and push your raft away from the floating carcass of the Crocodile. Unless you possess a Pouch of Unlimited Contents, into which you put them, your spear and your axe (if you have either of these) will have rolled off the raft during the battle with the Crocodile. You curse your loss, but push on up-river (turn to **390**).

32

By the time you have found all the prisoners and released them, you have become leader of sixty-three dedicated followers, eager for revenge (turn to **201**).

33

You soon reach the beach but duck back down behind the rocks when you see what is happening on it. A rowing-boat has been dragged on to the beach, obviously by the six PIRATES who are standing around a large chest. You look at Mungo and discuss what to do. If you wish to attack the Pirates, turn to **340**. If you would rather climb back to the inlet and over to the beach in the other cove, turn to **24**.

34

You carry on crawling down the tunnel but decide it is leading nowhere. There is not much room to turn, and you have to tuck your head between your legs and flip over. You scramble back down the bore-hole and are relieved to reach the main tunnel.

However, when you flipped over in the bore-hole something fell out of your backpack. Deduct one item from your Equipment List and lose 1 LUCK point. You clamber out of the bore-hole and turn left down the tunnel (turn to 321).

35
The words form a stark warning which reads 'Turn Back or Die'. But you cannot tell whether the warning is for those entering the gorge or for those leaving it, as the boulder faces both ways, equally. However, not wishing to take chances, you grip your sword and walk stealthily down the gorge (turn to 119).

36
The Lizard King closes in on you. Are you holding a fire sword as your weapon? If you are, turn to 111. If you must fight the Lizard King with an ordinary sword, turn to 346.

37
Although you are expecting some terrible beast to rise out of the water, everything remains calm. Gradually the ground becomes firmer underfoot and soon you are out of the water and walking through thick mud. Keeping a watchful eye on the terrain and sky, you are unaware of the disgusting soft bodies clinging to your legs. It is only when you notice some discomfort that you look down to see the GIANT LEECHES wrapped around your calves. Roll one die and add 1 to the number rolled.

This is the number of Giant Leeches clinging to you. Lose 1 STAMINA point for each and a portion of your Provisions: you need salt to get them off your leg. If you are still alive, turn to **280**.

38
The Lizard Man must be almost deaf as it does not hear your sword drop and continues walking up the tunnel. You pick up your sword and follow (turn to **51**).

39
The floor of the tunnel is strewn with rocks the size of coconuts. They are all surprisingly smooth. Some appear to move slightly, but you suspect it must be the dim light playing tricks on your eyes. Then suddenly one uncurls and shoots forward on tiny legs towards you, and you feel a sharp pain in your leg, as though teeth are tearing at your flesh. Lose 1 STAMINA point. You realize with horror that you are surrounded by GRANNITS, vicious armadillo-like man-eaters. If you have been bitten by a Rattlesnake, turn to **207**; if you have not, turn to **25**.

40
You walk down the gorge and into shadow, the sunlight being cut off by the southern hills. As the gorge narrows, you suddenly hear a rumbling above you. It is the sound of a landslide, and soon rocks and boulders are crashing down all around you. *Test your Luck*. If you are Lucky, turn to **253**. If you are Unlucky, turn to **107**.

41

Inside the snuff-box you find a small gold nugget and a piece of paper with a message scrawled in charcoal which reads: 'If you read this, it will mean that I have failed in my attempt to escape from the slave mines of the Lizard King. My raft is hidden beyond the gorge where the plain meets the river. If you are here to help us, please follow the river upstream until you see the mud huts. The slave mines are near by, but beware the Lizard Man guards.'

You fold up the piece of paper, put it in your pocket together with the gold nugget, and continue to follow the footprints (turn to 325).

42

With your sword raised high, you lunge at your nearest foe. It is a HOBGOBLIN.

HOBGOBLIN   SKILL 6   STAMINA 5

If you win, turn to 341.

43

The Lizard Men see you and react quickly. You must fight them both at once.

	SKILL	STAMINA
First LIZARD MAN	9	8
Second LIZARD MAN	8	8

During combat, both Lizard Men will have a separate attack on you in each Attack Round, but you must choose which of the two you will fight. Attack your nominated target as in a normal battle. Against the other you will throw for your Attack Strength in the normal way, but you will not wound it if your Attack Strength is greater – you must count this as though you have just parried its blow. Of course, if its Attack Strength is greater, it will have wounded you in the normal way. As soon as you have killed one of the Lizard Men and wounded the other twice, turn to **284**.

44

You soon arrive at another junction. Looking left, you see daylight at the end of the tunnel and remember that it is the entrance. You decide to walk straight past it (turn to **274**).

45

Your sword rebounds off the Lizard Man's armour. He whirls round to face his would-be assassin and thrusts at you with his scimitar.

TWO-HEADED
LIZARD MAN   SKILL 9   STAMINA 9

If you win, turn to **173**.

46

The man's eyes light up at the mention of food; he puts down his pole and beckons you to sit down. As he devours your offerings (lose 1 portion of your Provisions), you tell him of your quest. He tells you that he was once a thief on the mainland who was caught and sentenced by Prince Olaf to five years' imprisonment on Fire Island. After the Lizard Men began their rule of the island, he was forced to work in the gold mines. One day, however, he managed to escape and has lived in hiding in the jungle ever since. He thinks he is too old to brave a journey by raft to the mainland and is happy enough to live in his tree den. You ask him if he has any information which may be of use to you and he replies that he will willingly tell you all he knows in exchange for some more food. If you wish to give him another portion of your Provisions, turn to **149**. If you would rather threaten him, turn to **69**.

47

As you walk down the main tunnel, you pass a branch on your right and the entrance tunnel on your left. You come to the edge of a vertical downward shaft, to the side of which is secured a wooden ladder. You look down the shaft and although you cannot see the bottom, you decide to climb down (turn to **315**).

48

As you bend down to look at the strange eggs, one of them splits open. Clear, viscous liquid seeps out of the crack and then a hole appears in the side of the egg. You see a long jaw lined with spiked teeth poke through the hole followed by a smooth eyeless head, deep green in colour. The beast sniffs the air – and then instinctively leaps at your throat. You have unfortunately found the nest of a RAZORJAW, a hideous creature that has evolved to kill all other species. If you are wearing Sog's helmet, turn to 56; if you are not, turn to 304.

49

You sheathe your sword and set off west again. Gradually the ground becomes firmer underfoot, and soon you are out of the water and walking across a muddy plain. Ahead you see two hills and you decide to walk towards the gorge dividing them (turn to 362).

50

You charge at the door with your shoulder. Roll two dice. If the number rolled is less than or equal to your SKILL score, turn to 356. If the number rolled is greater than your SKILL, turn to 266.

51

The noise of singing voices and iron hitting rock is quite loud; you must be close to where the slaves are working. You decide to run quietly up behind the Lizard Man and deal with it. You pick up a large stone and run forward. The Lizard Man hears you – but too late to stop you from bringing the stone down hard on the back of its head. As it crashes to the floor you catch its pail, thinking it might contain much-needed water for the thirsty slaves. You walk on until the tunnel opens out into a chamber (turn to **223**).

52
The poison in the Giant Wasp's sting has affected your co-ordination. Lose 1 SKILL point. Turn to **141**.

53
A sweet smell floats down from the upper foliage of the tree which makes you feel relaxed and drowsy. As your eyelids droop, you do not see a thick vine lower itself down from the branches above. It silently wraps itself around your neck and starts to squeeze. You awaken, choking, and try to grasp your sword which is lying by your feet. *Test your Luck*. If you are Lucky, turn to **256**. If you are Unlucky, turn to **132**.

54
As you bend down to search the Lizard King's clothing, you see the Gonchong withdraw its proboscis from its host's forehead. It springs forward on its long legs in an attempt to land on your head. Roll two dice. If the total is the same or less than

your SKILL, turn to **244**. If the total is greater than your SKILL, turn to **260**.

55

Your constitution is strong, and the snake's venom does not affect you too badly. Lose 2 STAMINA points. You bandage the wound with a piece of cloth and rest awhile. If you wish to drive the Rattlesnake out of its hole with your sword, turn to **5**. If you would rather walk carefully down into the gorge to head west, turn to **119**.

56

You turn your head away from the leaping Razor-jaw which blindly crashes into the neck-guard of your helmet. It bounces off and you draw your sword to slay the vile thing.

RAZORJAW   SKILL 6   STAMINA 5

If you win, turn to **20**.

57

Back at the junction you may either turn left (to **361**) or continue straight along the tunnel (to **19**).

58

Sinking knee-deep in the slimy marsh, you struggle to keep up with the agile Marsh Hopper. Suddenly it turns south and once again beckons you to follow it. If you wish to keep following the Marsh Hopper, turn to **235**. If you wish to keep heading west, turn to **37**.

59

Climbing up the hill, your foot catches an unseen piece of twine tied between two small piles of rocks. The rocks tumble over, alerting the occupant of the cave to the presence of an intruder. A wild-eyed CAVE WOMAN appears at the mouth of the cave wearing furs and carrying a spear and a stone club. She steps forward and hurls her spear at you. *Test your Luck.* If you are Lucky, turn to **108**. If you are Unlucky, turn to **255**.

60

You miss all three of the quick-moving Grannits and must fight them one at a time.

	SKILL	STAMINA
First GRANNIT	4	3
Second GRANNIT	3	2
Third GRANNIT	4	3

If you win, turn to **192**.

61

You look round to see Mungo fighting the last remaining pirate – the captain! Before you can help him, the captain lunges forward, piercing poor Mungo through the chest. He lets out an anguished cry and drops on to the golden sand in a crumpled heap. The captain turns to face you, a grotesque sneer on his face, distorted by a long black scar running down the left side. You charge at the captain, seeking to avenge Mungo.

PIRATE CAPTAIN   SKILL 10   STAMINA 6

If you win, turn to **165**.

62

The pike misses you and the Hobgoblin runs away panic-stricken. You cross the archway quickly to stand on the other side of the ravine (turn to **139**).

63

Mud huts and Lizard Men guards; you realize that the gold mines must be near by! If you wish to walk past the huts to find the mines, turn to **147**. If you would rather deal with the Lizard Men first, turn to **329**.

64

Unknown to you, the ring also has a useful function. It helps its wearer to see through illusions. The maggots fade away before your eyes, the spell of the Shaman broken. You have passed the test. If you have now passed three tests, turn to **214**. If not, which will you try next?

Luck	Turn to **2**
Fear	Turn to **75**
Pain	Turn to **151**
Strength	Turn to **220**
Dexterity	Turn to **335**

65

You set off again, hoping to find the Shaman soon. You notice a few tufts of grass tied in knots and guess that he is not far away. You wonder if he knows you are near and stop to look around. There is no sign of life, merely a dead seagull lying on a rock to your right. If you have read the Shaman's chalk marks, turn to **89**. If you have not read his message, turn to **365**.

66

You pick up the chief's spear and run back into the jungle the way you came. You are soon well away from the village and slow down to a walk. Once again you are alone on your quest (turn to **113**).

67

The Shaman takes the bones from you and the pain immediately stops. However, you have failed the test and the Shaman will not now divulge his secrets. He points south-east, saying that the prison colony lies in that direction and that you must face the Gonchong without his help. You turn around and walk down the side of the volcano towards the Lizard King's stronghold (turn to **168**).

68

The tunnel is now very narrow and the beams supporting the roof are cracked and dislodged in places. You feel very claustrophobic in the dim light, but you press on, often being showered with dust and small stones. The tunnel ends again at another junction. Will you:

Turn left?	Turn to 278
Turn right?	Turn to 70
Turn back?	Turn to 172

69

The old thief jumps to his feet and climbs higher up the tree, cursing you out loud. He is very agile and you will not catch him up, carrying your backpack and sword. You decide to leave him alone and climb down the vine to continue north-west (turn to 375).

70

The tunnel makes a sharp right turn, continuing on as far as you can see. As you start to walk down it, you are suddenly stopped in your tracks by the sound of rumbling above you. A beam cracks and suddenly the whole ceiling comes crashing down on top of you. Lose 5 STAMINA points. If you are still alive, *Test your Luck*. If you are Lucky, turn to 345. If you are Unlucky, turn to 175.

71

As you continue to hack your way noisily through the lush vegetation, you are unaware of the six PYGMIES you have attracted, who are now following you. They surround you before coming into view, their blowpipes aimed at your exposed flesh. If you wish to communicate with them, turn to **276**. If you would rather fight them, turn to **359**.

72

The marks are a simple request, written by the Shaman you are seeking. They ask you to find a feather and tie it in your hair, if you wish peaceful contact with him. You wonder how the Shaman knows you are looking for him, and realize it is important to find a feather. You set off immediately to find one (turn to **30**).

73

Although you try to stab the Spit Toad as it leaps at you, your blade fails to find its mark. Terrified, you are knocked to the ground by the huge amphibian. Its spiked teeth sink into one of your arms. *Test your Luck*. If you are Lucky, turn to **217**. If you are Unlucky, turn to **396**.

74

The approaching Lizard Man is not suspicious of you and your gang of Dwarfs and you pass by without any trouble (turn to 114).

75

The Shaman walks over to you and touches your head with his fingertips. Your mind fills with terrible and threatening images, so real that you want to scream out in terror. Are you wearing red powder on your face? If you are, turn to 155. If you are not, turn to 131.

76

The spear flies through the air, striking you in the shoulder and sending you crashing to the ground. Lose 3 STAMINA points. If you are still alive, you see the man that you rescued come to your side and pull the spear from your shoulder. He picks you up and helps you run for cover inside one of the huts, as the other Headhunters turn to attack you. Inside the hut, the rescued man arms himself with a spear and a stone-headed club. His gratitude shows in a smile and suddenly he runs out of the hut, screaming at the top of his voice. You watch as he charges into a group of advancing Headhunters, stabbing and hacking at them in a mad frenzy. Before he finally succumbs to their blows, he manages to slay three of them. You stagger out of the hut to fight the remaining Headhunters, but only one, the chief, steps forward to fight; the others turn and flee.

CHIEF
HEADHUNTER   SKILL 8   STAMINA 8

If you win, turn to 66.

77

The door flies open and you see a Dwarf shackled by his arms and legs being pushed into the laboratory by a grotesque two-headed LIZARD MAN. It pushes the poor Dwarf towards the door leading to the storeroom. If you wish to leap out from your hiding-place to attack the mutant, turn to 289. If you would rather wait to come out after they have gone into the storeroom, turn to 91.

78

You crouch down in the darkest recess you can find in the wall. The footsteps draw nearer and then you see a LIZARD MAN carrying an iron pail. It walks past without noticing you, complaining to itself about the weight of the pail. You follow it down the tunnel at a safe distance. If you have drunk a Potion of Clumsiness, turn to **154**. If you have not drunk this potion, turn to **184**.

79

You walk up the hill and step inside the cave. It smells of rotten food and stale body odour. The few possessions are strewn all over the floor amidst the rubbish. You are about to leave the cave when you catch sight of a small clay bowl almost hidden in a recess beside the Cave Woman's fur bedding. The bowl contains red powder. Will you:

Dab some on your face?	Turn to **332**
Swallow some of it?	Turn to **97**
Leave the cave without touching it?	Turn to **17**

80

You cut off a bunch of bananas and climb back down the tree. The bananas are sweet and juicy. Add 2 STAMINA points. Feeling quite content, you crawl into your shelter to settle down for the night. Looking up, you see wispy clouds in shades of pink and purple gradually deepen in colour as night takes over from day. Despite the deafening noise of thousands of insects enjoying the cool night air, you are soon fast asleep. *Test your Luck*. If you are Lucky, turn to **388**. If you are Unlucky, turn to **348**.

81

As you push your way slowly through the under-growth, the hairs on the back of your neck start to prickle and you feel that you are being watched. You stand back, sword ready, watching the leaves for any sign of movement. Then three dark-skinned men step into view, each wearing only a crude loin-cloth. They are armed with stone clubs and long spears, but you are more alarmed to see that each wears a belt of shrunken human heads. The HEADHUNTERS start to argue about who should kill you and earn the right to wear your head on his belt. Finally one steps forward. Fight them one at a time.

	SKILL	STAMINA
First HEADHUNTER	6	6
Second HEADHUNTER	7	6
Third HEADHUNTER	6	7

If you win, turn to **177**.

82

You run up the staircase until you reach a wooden door. Turning the handle slowly, you open it slightly. There, in the open air, standing feet astride on the battlement, is the infamous LIZARD KING waving a clenched fist and calling to his troops. A strange BLACK LION sits obediently at his side, but it is the sight of the Gonchong on the Lizard King's head that makes you tremble. You breathe in deeply and step out on to the battlements. You wave to your own troops and call out to the Lizard King. He does not even bother to look at you, and merely snaps his fingers to send the Black Lion bounding at you.

BLACK LION   SKILL 11   STAMINA 11

If you win, turn to **203**.

83

The side of the hill is quite steep and you lose your footing on some scree. You tumble over and slide down the hill. *Test your Luck*. If you are Lucky, turn to **334**. If you are Unlucky, turn to **281**.

84

The door opens into a corridor which runs left and right. Looking right, the corridor comes to a dead end, so you turn left. There is another door in the right-hand wall with the word 'Jailer' painted on it. Further ahead, the corridor turns sharply left where it meets a spiral staircase. If you wish to open the door, turn to **195**. If you would rather walk on to the staircase, turn to **8**.

85

As each of the other three Grannits run at you, you try to cleave their bony shells before they sink their teeth into your leg. Roll one die. If you roll 1 or 2, turn to **60**. If you roll 3 or 4, turn to **239**. If you roll 5 or 6, turn to **112**.

86

The Pygmies look surprised at your audacity and begin to laugh. One of them steps forward and offers you some nuts and berries. If you wish to eat them, turn to **18**. If you do not wish to eat them, turn to **295**.

87

As soon as you are close enough, the man leaps on to your raft. His eyes look wild and he is sweating profusely. He is delirious with fever and it is impossible to communicate with him. Suddenly he pulls a dagger from his clothing and tries to stab you. You do not have time to draw your sword and are forced to fight him with your bare hands.

DELIRIOUS
PRISONER   SKILL 6   STAMINA 5

During each Attack Round you must reduce your Attack Strength by 3 because you are fighting empty-handed. As soon as you win your second Attack Round, turn to 130.

88

You decide to build a raft and punt your way up-river. The river is not very deep and you have no difficulty in wading across it to some small trees on the far bank. If you possess an axe, turn to 179. If you do not have an axe, turn to 305.

89

You walk over to the seagull and pluck a feather from its wing. Using twine from your backpack, you tie the feather to the back of your head and walk on feeling a little self-conscious (turn to 269).

90

The old man pulls a piece of bent wire out of his pocket and proudly hands it to you. He sees the puzzled expression on your face and explains, 'It's a picklock's wire and I used it to unlock my leg irons before escaping from the mines. It might come in handy if you are captured.' You thank the old man and climb down the vine to continue north-west (turn to **375**).

91

As soon as the mutant and his prisoner have left the laboratory, you crawl out from under the bench and walk through the open doorway ahead (turn to **180**).

92

The water is refreshing to drink. Add 1 STAMINA point. While drinking, you notice a wooden casket lying on the bottom of the pool. If you wish to wade into the pool to reach the casket, turn to **259**. If you would rather head off west again, turn to **222**.

93

You take careful aim and release the dagger. It flies perfectly straight and sinks into the orange, knocking it off the rock. You have passed the test. If you have now passed three tests, turn to **214**. If not, which will you try next?

Luck	Turn to **2**
Fear	Turn to **75**
Pain	Turn to **151**
Revulsion	Turn to **183**
Strength	Turn to **220**

94

The boots fit your feet perfectly. You run around in a circle but nothing good or untoward happens, so you decide to leave them on. If you have not done so already, you may:

Drink the liquid in the phial	Turn to **311**
Open the pouch	Turn to **26**
Put the ring on your finger	Turn to **297**

If you do not wish to do any of these things, you may continue your way west again across the grassy plain (turn to **222**).

95

The mutant Lizard Man jumps off the dead Styraco-saurus and lumbers over to you with his halberd outstretched.

MUTANT LIZARD
MAN   SKILL 9   STAMINA 9

If you win, turn to **133**.

96

You stand on guard, waiting for the other Pygmies to attack. But they simply pick up their dead com-rade and vanish into the undergrowth in silence. Once again you are left alone to continue your journey west (turn to **7**).

97

The powder is almost impossible to swallow. You inhale some into your lungs and start to cough. It feels as if your lungs are burning. Lose 2 STAMINA points and 1 LUCK point. Eventually the pain sub-sides. Will you now either dab some powder on your face (turn to **332**) or leave the cave without the powder (turn to **17**).

98

Slowly but surely you lift the huge boulder off the ground. The Shaman signals for you to drop it, satisfied with your strength. You have passed the test. If you have now passed three tests, turn to **214**. If not, which will you try next?

Luck	Turn to **2**
Fear	Turn to **75**
Pain	Turn to **151**
Revulsion	Turn to **183**
Dexterity	Turn to **335**

99

The Ogre is not carrying anything of use to you and so you carry on building your raft. About an hour later you finally have enough logs to make a small raft. You tie them together with vines and drag your raft into the river. Using a long thin branch, you are soon punting your way up-river (turn to **387**).

100

The fruit is juicy and tastes delicious. Add 1 STAMINA point. Feeling refreshed, you set off again, still wiping the sticky juice from around your mouth. *Test your Luck.* If you are Lucky, turn to **352**. If you are Unlucky, turn to **160**.

101

You see a hand-cart with wooden wheels lying on its side in the middle of the tunnel, blocking your way. A short broken skeletal body, perhaps that of a Dwarf, lies beside it. A round bore-hole opens out into the tunnel and you wonder whether a Rock Grub might have attacked the unfortunate Dwarf. The tunnel continues on as far as you can see, although there is no sign of life ahead. If you wish to crawl down the bore-hole, turn to **10**. If you wish to climb over the cart and continue down the tunnel, turn to **321**.

102

You run back through the undergrowth the way you came, oblivious of the sharp branches and thorns cutting into you. Ahead you see a hollow log, into which you think you might be able to squeeze. If you wish to risk hiding in the log, turn to **16**. If you wish to keep on running, turn to **169**.

103

Although the itching is almost unbearable, something worse is happening. You break out in a sweat and then start to shiver. You are in the early stages of malaria. Lose 3 STAMINA points. If you are still alive, check your STAMINA. If it is 12 or above, turn to **15**. If it is 11 or below, turn to **316**.

104

You stand up and look inside your backpack. Your Provisions (if you have any remaining) have disintegrated and are no longer edible, but all your other possessions are still intact. You have no choice but to continue your journey on foot (turn to 197).

105

Being very wary of the vegetation, you stay alert, constantly looking about. Half-way up a tree to your left you see a crude platform and a vine hanging down from it. If you wish to climb up to the platform, turn to 286. If you would rather press on, turn to 375.

106

After saying a few words, you realize that the girl cannot understand you. Perhaps she was left on Fire Island as a child and has become as wild as the animals. She cowers back, uttering a few sounds to the Tiger. It is obviously wise to leave her alone and so you back off slowly, hoping not to scare her. At a safe distance you turn and walk quickly into the valley to reconnoitre with the freed slaves (turn to 279).

107

The boulders fall down like rain, and inevitably one hits you. Roll one die. If you roll 1 or 2, turn to 210. If you roll 3 or 4, turn to 336. If you roll 5 or 6, turn to 245.

108

The spear whistles past your head, clattering on to the rocks behind you. The Cave Woman grunts in anger and runs forward to attack you with her club.

CAVE WOMAN   SKILL 5   STAMINA 5

If you win, turn to **79**.

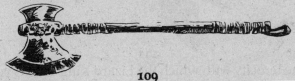

109

You put your lips to the mouthpiece of the horn and blow as hard as you can. The tide of the battle suddenly turns as your companions rally to the sound of the horn. A gap appears in the ranks of the Lizard King's troops as they fall back, and you run through. You reach the wooden gates of the fort, and run through them into the inner courtyard. If you wish to walk through the double doors in the wall to your left, turn to **268**. If you would rather try the doors straight ahead in the far wall, turn to **84**.

110

Not only is your skin allergic to the fungus spores, but your stomach does not take kindly to it either. You are violently sick, as the fungus you have eaten is poisonous. Lose 3 STAMINA points and 1 LUCK point. If you are still alive, you gradually begin to feel better and set off again through the undergrowth (turn to **224**).

111

The ferocity with which the Lizard King attacks you is staggering. Blow after blow of his fire sword crashes down on you and it is all you can do to defend yourself.

LIZARD KING   SKILL 12   STAMINA 15

If you win, turn to **153**.

112

You manage to stop two of the quick-moving Grannits, but must fight the remaining one.

GRANNIT   SKILL 4   STAMINA 3

If you win, turn to **192**.

113

Slowly you hack your way through the dense jungle, not really certain of the direction in which you are heading. Later, you catch a brief glimpse of the sun through the trees, enough to orientate yourself, and turn to head west (turn to **7**).

114

The Dwarfs walk quickly through the tunnels, their knowledge of the complex network acquired through months of slavery. They finally come to a halt and one of them whispers to you that another group of prisoners is working around the next bend. You hear the dull sounds of picks and hammers hitting rock and tell the Dwarfs that they should walk on and that you will signal to them the moment they should attack the prisoners' guards. They walk round the bend and you see a group of men and Elves chained together working at a rockface. Two ORC GUARDS are yelling at them to work faster. They look surprised to see you but do not see through your disguise until you are almost alongside them. They scream a battle-cry and draw their swords. *Test your Luck*. If you are Lucky, turn to **265**. If you are Unlucky, turn to **138**.

115

The spear skewers the pig and brings it to an abrupt halt. You gather some wood and build a fire, eager to roast the pig. When it is finally cooked, you sit down on the ground to enjoy a much-needed feast. Add 3 STAMINA points. With your strength renewed, you set off west again (turn to **170**).

116

The food is very appetizing and you sit down to enjoy it. Add 2 STAMINA points. As you are finishing the last of it, you suddenly hear a rustling in the bushes behind you. There was a good reason for the owner of the food to hang it in the tree: to keep it out of reach of the BEAR which is about to attack you.

BEAR   SKILL 10   STAMINA 9

If you win, turn to **247**. You may *Escape* after two Attack Rounds by running away from the Bear (turn to **27**).

117

As you continue your climb, the old man jumps into defensive action. A barrage of coconuts is hurled down at you, and although you tell him that you mean no harm, he continues throwing down whatever is to hand, shrieking 'Go away!' at the top of his voice. By the time you reach the platform, you have a few painful lumps on your head (lose 1 STAMINA point). Now you see the man at the far side of the sheltered platform, standing nervously with a bamboo pole in his hands, wearing nothing but canvas shorts. Will you:

Offer him some of your Provisions?	Turn to **46**
Leave him alone and continue north-west through the undergrowth?	Turn to **375**
Step on the platform and pull his bamboo pole away from him?	Turn to **349**

118

You fall back, clutching madly at the air, to land heavily on the ground. Lose 1 STAMINA point. You climb back up the tree immediately, flicking the Tarantula off with your sword. Turn to **80**.

119

In the fine sand on the ground you notice traces of old footprints leading out of the gorge. They end abruptly in front of you, and there are signs of a struggle. Two pairs of footprints lead back down the gorge, with two straight lines behind them as though their owners have dragged a body behind them. As you follow the trail of the footprints, you catch sight of a shiny object in the sand. You prod it with your foot and see an oval snuff-box made of brass. Picking it up you see that it has a hinged lid. If you wish to open the snuff-box, turn to **41**. If you would rather throw it back into the dust and continue to follow the footprints, turn to **325**.

120

The word 'Gonchong' strikes fear into the Hobgoblin. He shrieks in terror and hurls his pike at you. *Test your Luck*. If you are Lucky, turn to **62**. If you are Unlucky, turn to **240**.

121

The Elves and men cheer when the second Orc is slain. The Dwarfs break their chains and now you have fourteen friends to help you finish your quest. One of them is from Oyster Bay, and despite his joy at the prospect of freedom, he is saddened by the news of Mungo's death. Armed with their own tools of slavery, the prisoners ask you to lead them to attack the stone fort used as the prison camp where the Lizard King still resides, protected by his mutant slaves and élite guards. You agree to do so and set off again through the tunnels to release the rest of the slave miners. Roll one die. If you roll 1 or 2, turn to **251**. If you roll 3 or 4, turn to **293**. If you roll 5 or 6, turn to **32**.

122

You wipe the thick blood off your sword and trudge off west again, wondering what other creatures might be lurking in the black waters of the marshland. Turn to **37**.

123

Despite the Lizard King's terror, the Gonchong forces him to attack you with his lethal fire sword. Frightened by the flame, your monkey jumps off your shoulder and disappears. The Lizard King immediately attacks you with staggering ferocity, now that his fear is gone (turn to **346**).

124

The snake's venom is too strong for your system to endure and you lose consciousness. *Test your Luck*. If you are Lucky, turn to **156**. If you are Unlucky, turn to **357**.

125

You are about to pass out from the pain when the Shaman steps forward and takes the bones from you. You have passed the test. If you have now passed three tests, turn to **214**. If not, which will you try next?

Luck	Turn to **2**
Fear	Turn to **75**
Revulsion	Turn to **183**
Strength	Turn to **220**
Dexterity	Turn to **335**

126

You reach into your backpack and take out three portions of your Provisions and divide them among the Pygmies. They each smell the food before trying it. They look at each other and all stop chewing at once. They spit out the food, noisily expressing their disgust. One of them signals to the others to attack you, but just as he pulls his stone club from his belt, he falls over clutching his stomach. The others too begin to stagger; your food has made them ill. You waste no more time and head off west into the undergrowth as fast as you can (turn to 7).

127

The Hobgoblin is obviously very stupid as he believes you to be one of the Lizard King's guards. He thrusts out his pike and says in a deep voice, 'What is the password?' What will you reply?

'What?'   Turn to 193
'Gonchong.'   Turn to 120
'Fire Island.'   Turn to 287

128

The water in the pool looks cool and refreshing, although you are a little perturbed at the layer of green algae which floats on the surface. As you bend down to drink, a jet of liquid shoots out of the pond towards you from a wide green mouth which suddenly appears in the water. Roll two dice. If the number rolled is the same or less than your SKILL, turn to 248. If the number rolled is greater than your SKILL, turn to 351.

129

You grab the pole from the medicine man, but at the same instant it becomes an iron bar, as hot as if it had just been pulled from a blacksmith's fire. Lose 2 STAMINA points, 1 SKILL point and 1 LUCK point for your foolish aggression towards the powerful Shaman. You drop the iron bar on the ground, staring at it in disbelief. If you now wish to talk to the Shaman, turn to 324. If you would rather attack him with your sword, turn to 157.

130

You punch the man full in the face and knock him into the river. He screams but does not try to climb back on to the raft. You feel guilty about leaving him behind, but you must press ahead with your mission (turn to 14).

131

Your mind is out of control and you are unable to stop yourself from screaming out. You have failed the test and the Shaman will not now divulge his secrets. The vile images fade away and the Shaman points south-east, saying that the prison colony lies in that direction and that you must face the Gonchong without his help. You turn around and walk down the side of the volcano towards the Lizard King's stronghold (turn to 168).

132

You stretch out as far as you can but are unable to reach your sword. The vine's grip becomes tighter and tighter and you soon lose consciousness. You have fallen prey to a carnivorous tree.

133

The mutant has a shield which you decide to take, as it is light yet strong. Add 1 SKILL point. The prison colony cannot be too far away and you waste no more time in setting off again (turn to 218).

134

Gradually your vision returns and you sheathe your sword. If you still wish to drink at the pool, turn to **92**. If you would rather head off west again, turn to **222**.

135

At the junction you may either continue straight on (turn to **39**) or turn right (turn to **361**).

136

You put the whip in your belt and decide what to do next. If you wish to pick up a rusty knife, turn to **275**. If you would rather head directly over to the door in the far wall, turn to **312**.

137

You gesticulate to the Pygmies, to tell them that you will not give them anything. They look annoyed and each blows a dart at you. Roll one die to determine the number of darts that stick into your flesh and deduct 1 STAMINA point for each. If you are still alive, turn to **373**.

138

One of the Orcs swings at you with its sword and you must fight it.

ORC GUARD   SKILL 7   STAMINA 7

If you win, turn to **121**. You may *Escape* by backing off towards the Dwarfs (turn to **11**).

139

Once again you head off south-east, walking over sand and rock. Riding towards you on a dinosaur-like steed is a heavily armoured reptilian. It is a mutant LIZARD MAN riding a STYRACOSAUR-US. The Lizard Man urges his mount into a trot to attack you.

STYRACOSAURUS   SKILL 11   STAMINA 10

If you win, turn to **95**.

140

You fall on to the floor, but do not injure yourself. You stand up but do not get much further as the tunnel comes to a dead end. You have no option but to return to the last junction (turn to **378**).

141

You set off again in search of the Shaman (turn to **399**).

142

You look over your shoulder as you run, to see if the girl and her Tiger are giving chase. Fortunately, they are nowhere to be seen. You slow down and walk down the valley to reconnoitre with the freed slaves (turn to **279**).

143

You pluck a few lush leaves from a funnel-shaped plant and rub them furiously on to your lumpy face.

The relief is instantaneous and the itching mercifully stops. If you still wish to eat the fungus, turn to **110**. If you would rather set off again through the undergrowth, turn to **224**.

144

Your sword pierces the heart of the Lizard Man, killing it instantly (turn to **173**).

145

As you slowly put your hand into the hole, fear grips you on hearing a familiar rattling sound. You try to retract your hand before the fangs of the RATTLESNAKE sink into your arm, but it is too quick: its poison is in your blood. You waste no time and cut the wound with your own sword to draw the blood. If your STAMINA score is 18 or below, turn to **264**. If it exceeds 18, turn to **55**.

146

The bush has poison-tipped thorns. Lose 3 STAM-
INA points. If you are still alive, you stagger on
resolutely towards the prison colony (turn to **291**).

147

Behind the huts, a path leads through the trees to
the rocky face of a steep hill. In the centre of the
rock-face you see the square shape of a mine entrance leading into the hill. There are many footprints leading in and out of the mine. You step
carefully inside, keeping close to the wall. The
tunnel is lit by torches which cast eerie shadows all
around. You sense that you are walking downhill,
and soon arrive at a junction. If you wish to turn left,
turn to **274**. If you wish to turn right, turn to **28**.

148

Not far away from your shelter you find a cluster of
banana trees. The fruit is out of reach and you have
to climb up to get it. *Test your Luck*. If you are Lucky,
turn to **80**. If you are Unlucky, turn to **13**.

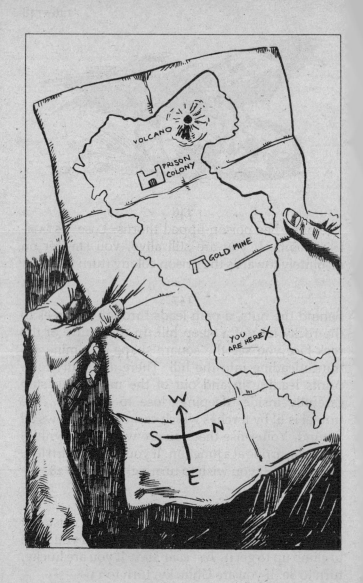

149

The old man takes the food and begins to draw a rough map of the island on a piece of cloth with some charcoal. He points to where you are now and also marks the sites of the mine and prison colony which is where the Lizard King lives. You fold the map up and put it in your backpack. Just as you are about to climb down the vine, the old man says, 'And for just a little bit more of your delicious food I will give you something really useful.' If you wish to give him yet another portion of your Provisions, turn to **90**. If you would rather climb down and continue north-west, turn to **375**.

150

You somehow manage to escape the raging torrent and fall breathless on to the right-hand bank. The Water Elemental's fury subsides behind you as you lie exhausted in the mud. *Test your Luck*. If you are Lucky, turn to **104**. If you are Unlucky, turn to **159**.

151

The Shaman hands you his two bones, telling you to hold one in each hand. All your muscles immediately start to bulge and then you feel as though your insides are expanding. You believe you are going to burst and the pain is excruciating. If you beg the Shaman to stop the pain, turn to **67**. If you grit your teeth and try to bear the pain, turn to **125**.

152

Behind the hut you see a narrow goat-track leading up the side of the cliff. You wend your way up it and are quite exhausted by the time you reach the top. You take a swig of water from your flask and realize that water shortage could be a problem for you on this island. Looking west you see the daunting sight of the sleeping volcano standing above the trees, but no sign of life – although you can certainly hear it; a cacophony of bird and insect noise. With the light quickly fading, you decide to camp for the night behind some rocks. You do not sleep very well and are awake at first light, eager to set off. You decide to head directly west into the trees (turn to **391**).

153

Your last fatal blow sends the Lizard King crashing on to the stone floor. Will you:

Turn to salute your troops?	Turn to **188**
Sever the Gonchong's proboscis?	Turn to **384**
Search through the Lizard King's clothing?	Turn to **54**

154

You stumble over a stone on the floor and drop your sword as you try to stop yourself from falling. *Test your Luck*. If you are Lucky, turn to **38**. If you are Unlucky, turn to **319**.

155

The magical properties of the red powder help you to control your mind and you gradually overcome the terrible nightmare. You have passed the test. If you have now passed three tests, turn to **214**. If not, which will you try next?

Luck	Turn to **2**
Pain	Turn to **151**
Revulsion	Turn to **183**
Strength	Turn to **220**
Dexterity	Turn to **335**

156

Although you come close to death, you survive the snake's venom. However, the poison has seriously weakened you. Eventually, you regain consciousness and rest, but your attributes now consist of a SKILL score of 5 and a STAMINA score of 4. If you wish to drive the Rattlesnake out of its hole with your sword, turn to **5**. If you would rather walk carefully down into the gorge to head west, turn to **119**.

157

It is a fatal mistake to attack the powerful medicine man. A simple chant from his lips turns your sword into a writhing SERPENT which wraps itself around your arm. You scream in terror and try to shake it off. Your brief struggle is futile as the Serpent's fangs are filled with deadly poison which kills you almost instantly.

158

The ground under your feet becomes softer and softer, until with each step you are sinking into black mire up to your knees. It is very tiring to keep going, and you begin to worry; the whole landscape is water-covered with only the occasional clump of reeds breaking the surface. Still, you press on re-solutely until brought up short by the sight of a flaying tentacled arm unfolding out of the black water in front of you. Another arm reaches out before a hideous octopus-like beast with dark-green lumpy skin rises slowly into the air on its six arms. It is the loathsome SLIME SUCKER and you must fight it. If you have a spear, turn to **394**. If you do not have a spear, you must fight it with your sword.

SLIME SUCKER   SKILL 10   STAMINA 9

During each Attack Round you must reduce your Attack Strength by 2, because of your tiredness and lack of mobility. If you win, turn to **122**.

159

Although you were too concerned with swimming for your life to notice, the force of the water ripped your backpack off your back. All your Provisions and possessions have been washed away. Lose 2 LUCK points. Fortunately, your sword remains in its scabbard. You have no choice but to continue your journey on foot (turn to 197).

160

You hear buzzing above you and look up to see a GIANT WASP diving down at you, attracted by the sweet scent of the fruit juice. You draw your sword just in time to defend yourself.

GIANT WASP   SKILL 6   STAMINA 6

If you win without losing any Attack Rounds, turn to 141. If you win but have lost at least one Attack Round during combat, turn to 52.

161

Taking the Lizard Man's cloak to disguise yourself, you form the Dwarfs into a line so that it appears that you are a guard in charge of a chain gang of slaves. You crack the whip with a smile and set off down the tunnel. You follow the Dwarfs down endless tunnels, deeper and deeper into the mine. As you pass by another tunnel branch, you see a Lizard Man walking along it towards you. *Test your Luck.* If you are Lucky, turn to **74**. If you are Unlucky, turn to **262**.

162

No amount of tugging at the handle is going to open the door. If you wish to try to charge it down, turn to **50**. If you would rather walk back into the courtyard and try to open the other doors leading off it, turn to **84**.

163

The Lizard Men see you and react quickly. You must fight them both at the same time.

	SKILL	STAMINA
First LIZARD MAN	9	8
Second LIZARD MAN	8	8

During combat, both Lizard Men will have a separate attack on you in each Attack Round, but you must choose which of the two you will fight. Attack your nominated target as in a normal battle. Against the other, you will throw for your Attack Strength in the normal way, but you will not wound it if your Attack Strength is greater – you must count this as though you have just parried its blow. Of course if its Attack Strength is greater, it will have wounded you in the normal way. If you win, turn to 368.

164

The Goblin merely grunts in his sleep and does not wake up. You leave the room quietly, taking the breastplate with you. You try it on in the corridor and just manage to squeeze into it. Add 1 SKILL point. You close the Goblin's door and walk to the spiral staircase (turn to 8).

165

The sand all around Mungo is red with blood. You kneel down beside him and gently lift his head in your arms. His eyes open a little and he manages a half-smile despite his agony. In a whisper he says, 'Well, we got them, but a lot of good it did me. Make sure you get the Lizard King for me, won't you?' Then his eyes close and he slumps down dead. You bury him on the beach near the cliff, marking the grave with his sword skewered into the sand. You see a narrow goat-track leading up the side of the cliff and then look back at the chest lying on the beach. If you wish to walk up the goat-track, turn to **200**. If you wish to open the chest, turn to **398**.

166

As you enter his cell, you are surprised that the old man remains silent. If you are wearing a Ring of Confusion, turn to **294**. If you are not wearing this ring, turn to **318**.

167

You run after the pig waving your sword in the air, but it is too agile. It scurries off across the plain and is soon out of view. You slow down to walking pace and continue west still thinking about the succulent roast dinner you might have had (turn to **170**).

168

You walk quickly south-east, eager to meet up with the freed slaves. You soon arrive at the edge of a ravine which is too wide for you to jump over. You walk east, infuriated by the time you are wasting. Ahead you see a stone arch traversing the ravine, but an armoured HOBGOBLIN is standing guard by it. Will you:

Try to bluff your way across the stone archway?	Turn to 127
Offer him a gold nugget (if you have one) to let you cross?	Turn to 252
Attack him with your sword?	Turn to 328

169

The Headhunters are more adept at running through the jungle than you, and are quickly catching up. You decide to turn and fight. Fortunately, the path through the undergrowth is too narrow for more than one Headhunter to fight you at once.

	SKILL	STAMINA
First HEADHUNTER	7	5
Second HEADHUNTER	6	6
Third HEADHUNTER	6	7

Fight them one at a time, and if you win, turn to 261.

170

In the distance you see rising ground, and, beyond in the north-west, the ever-daunting shape of the sleeping volcano. It is not long before you reach the bushy bank of a river running slowly south-east. On the far side the ground is quite steep and tree-covered. If you have read the message in the snuff-box, turn to **288**. If you have not read this message, turn to **88**.

171

You crawl towards the fire, hoping that the Headhunters will be too engrossed in their ritual to notice you. *Test your Luck*. If you are Lucky, turn to **215**. If you are Unlucky, turn to **302**.

172

You are soon back at another junction. If you wish to keep walking straight ahead, turn to **383**. If you wish to turn right, turn to **4**.

173

The Dwarf shouts for joy as the Lizard Man slumps to the floor. If you have a picklock's wire, turn to **393**. If you do not own this thief's tool, turn to **216**.

174

The paste tastes bitter and your mouth starts to go numb. Your body begins to glow and you feel full of energy. Add 2 STAMINA points. You grab your sword and start to hack your way west again, with renewed vigour (turn to **113**).

175

You manage to crawl out backwards from underneath the rubble. You dust yourself down and walk back to the last junction; you cannot go forward because the tunnel is blocked. Back at the junction, you may either turn left (turn to **172**), or head straight on (turn to **278**).

176

The Shaman starts to shake his feathered pole which makes a rattling sound. He presumes you are an enemy, as you have not displayed your sign of friendship. Will you:

Try to talk to him?	Turn to **324**
Try to knock the feathered pole out of his hand?	Turn to **129**
Attack him with your sword?	Turn to **157**

177

The Headhunters have no items of equipment on them, but have a hide bag containing bananas and coconuts. You save your own Provisions and eat the Headhunters' food. Add 1 STAMINA point. You wonder if their village is nearby, and decide to climb a tree to get a better view. From the top you see smoke rising not far away in the south-west; perhaps from a village. Directly west, you see the trees gradually thin out, and away in the far north-west, you see the daunting shape of the volcano.

You climb down from the tree and plan which way to head. If you wish to keep going west, turn to **229**. If you wish to go north-west in order to circumvent the smoke, turn to **12**.

178

On a level piece of ground you see a circle of polished stones which contains a pile of artefacts: a bracelet, a clay doll, a tin mug and a buckle are just some of the things lying on the ground. Perhaps it is a collection place for gifts to the Shaman from his visitors. If you wish to place one of your own items in the stone circle, turn to **233**. If you would rather take any of the items from the circle, turn to **306**.

179

It does not take you long to chop down enough trees to make a small raft. You tie the logs together with vines and drag your raft into the river. Using a long thin branch, you are soon punting your way up-river (turn to **387**).

180

You find yourself in a corridor which turns sharply to the right. On the corner is a spiral staircase winding up the centre of a tower. You have a feeling that you should climb up the staircase (turn to **82**).

181

It is a slim chance, but you decide to try and capture the Water Elemental in your magical pouch. You open it as wide as possible and wait for the Water

Elemental to come crashing down on top of you. *Test your Luck*. If you are Lucky, turn to **230**. If you are Unlucky, turn to **257**.

182

You run at the Giant Crab with your sword drawn. It drops Mungo into the sand in order to attack you with both pincers.

GIANT CRAB   SKILL 10   STAMINA 11

If you win, turn to **366**.

183

The Shaman taps you with the end of his pole and suddenly your whole body is crawling with maggots. You feel them writhing around inside your mouth and ears. If you are wearing a Ring of Confusion, turn to **64**. If you are not wearing this ring, turn to **283**.

184

You stumble over a stone on the floor but manage to stop yourself from falling over and making any noise. Add 1 LUCK point. You breathe a sigh of relief and continue to follow the Lizard Man (turn to **51**).

185

With your sword raised high, you lunge at your nearest foe. It is a mutant LIZARD MAN.

MUTANT LIZARD
MAN   SKILL 9   STAMINA 8

If you win, turn to **341**.

186

As you reach into your backpack, you are almost trembling with hunger. You devour a portion of your Provisions and crawl into your shelter to settle down for the night. Looking up, you see wispy clouds in shades of pink and purple gradually deepen in colour as the night sky takes over from the day. Despite the deafening noise of thousands of insects enjoying the cool night air, you are soon fast asleep. *Test your Luck*. If you are Lucky, turn to **388**. If you are Unlucky, turn to **348**.

187

The bag contains merely a few broad leaves wrapped in small bundles. You squeeze the bundles and they feel as if they contain some paste or dough. You unwrap the leaves and find a bright green paste inside. Will you:

Rub some of the paste into your wounds?	Turn to 377
Eat some of the paste?	Turn to 174
Leave the paste and head off west again?	Turn to 113

188

Turning your back on the dreaded Gonchong is a mistake. Your troops hardly have time to enjoy the slaying of the Lizard King before the Gonchong withdraws its proboscis and jumps on to your head. Its needle-like proboscis skewers itself through your forehead and implants itself in your brain. You are now controlled by the Gonchong and can only watch helplessly as the Lizard King's army annihilates your demoralized troops. The battle is lost.

189

Before the unconscious Lizard Man comes round, you rummage through its pockets and find three iron keys which you put in your own pocket. You then tie its arms together behind its back and drag it into the hut. As soon as it regains consciousness, you demand information about the slave mines. It replies that the entrance to the mines is not far away – about a hundred metres beyond the huts. You tie the Lizard Man to a post and leave the hut to find the mines (turn to 147).

190

As soon as you touch the hilt of your sword, the native girl lets go of the rope. The Tiger is on top of you in one leap and you lose the first Attack Round. If you are still alive, you manage to draw your sword to defend yourself.

SABRE-TOOTHED
TIGER   SKILL 11   STAMINA 8

If you win, turn to 343.

191

Your hands are slippery with mud: you miss the huge Slime Sucker, and the spear falls harmlessly into the water. Now you must fight the Slime Sucker with your sword alone.

SLIME SUCKER   SKILL 10   STAMINA 9

If you win, turn to 122.

192

You decide to walk on down the tunnel, but you soon arrive at a dead end. You have no option but to turn round and walk back to the junction (turn to 57).

193

The Hobgoblin stares at you dumbly and says, 'Yes, that's right, "What" *is* the password. You may cross.' He steps to the side and you walk quickly over the archway to the other side of the ravine (turn to **139**).

194

You walk along the side of the hill following the route of the gorge. Looking over to the hill on the far side of the gorge, you suddenly see a landslide start, sending rocks and boulders crashing into the gorge. Although you are not enjoying the tiring climb, you are relieved that you were not in the gorge. Add 1 LUCK point. If you still wish to walk along the side of the hill above the gorge, turn to **83**. If you now wish to risk walking down the gorge, turn to **382**.

195

The door opens into a dingy room. Sunlight streams through a single barred window in the far wall. A straw mattress fills one corner of the room on which there lies a GOBLIN snoring heavily. An iron breastplate hangs on a nail over his bed. If you wish to tiptoe into the room to steal the breastplate, turn to 333. If you would rather close the door and walk to the spiral staircase, turn to 8.

196

You step round the huge body of the Giant Lizard and press on down the gorge. At last the gorge widens out to become a grassy plain, and the hills are soon behind you. Not far away, some ten metres to your left, you see a pond where many birds are drinking. If you want to drink at the pond, turn to 128. If you would rather continue west, turn to 222.

197

Looking west, you see the sun slowly sinking until it looks like a big red balloon sitting on the sea. Soon it will be dark and so you decide to camp down for the night between two rocks which you cover over with branches and leaves. You are very hungry after your ordeal in the river and realize that you must eat something soon. If you have any Provisions left, turn to **186**. If you do not have any food left, turn to **148**.

198

The abandoned hut is littered with broken furniture, smashed pottery and a few bits of torn clothing. You kick away a dirty rug and see the handle of a trapdoor in the floorboards. If you wish to lift the trapdoor, turn to **267**. If you would rather leave the hut, turn to **152**.

199

The Shaman listens intently as you explain about the Lizard King and your mission to destroy him. You tell him that you wish to know how to kill the parasitic Gonchong, thus reducing the Lizard King's power. The Shaman jumps in the air on hearing the word Gonchong, obviously not realizing that there was one on the island. In fractured sentences the Shaman explains that for him to share some of his secret magic with you, you must first earn the right, no matter how noble your mission is. He tells you that the test will be disturbing and painful. If you agree to the Shaman's terms, turn to

397. If you would rather face the Lizard King without the Shaman's knowledge, turn to **237**.

200

You wend your way up the goat-track and are quite exhausted by the time you reach the top. You take a swig of water from your flask and realize that water shortage could be a problem for you on this island. Looking west, you see the daunting sight of the sleeping volcano standing above the trees, but no sign of life – although you can certainly hear it: a cacophony of bird and insect noise. With the light quickly fading you decide to camp down for the night behind some rocks. You do not sleep very well and are awake at first light, eager to set off. You decide to head directly west into the trees (turn to **391**).

201

You lead your band of fighters out of the mines and attack the mud huts where the guards live. The last of them is soon slain and the former prisoners begin to celebrate by cheering and singing. An old Dwarf begins a jig and is soon encircled by a clapping, happy audience. For the moment, all sufferings and troubles are forgotten. While everybody is still revelling in their freedom, an Elf comes up to you and asks to speak with you alone. You walk away from the others to listen to what the Elf has to say. With a worried expression on his face, he tells you that an attack on the Lizard King's fort would be suicidal. For the sake of power and near-immortality, the

Lizard King has allowed a hideous parasite, the Gonchong, to attach itself to his head. With the Gonchong's proboscis implanted firmly in his brain, the Lizard King remains invincible, telepathically controlling his mutant warriors. To kill the Lizard King, the Gonchong must first be destroyed. But only the island's Shaman knows the secret of its magical powers. It cannot be harmed without the knowledge of how to break the link with its host. Alas, the Elf has never seen the Shaman in his four years on the island. Shamans lead solitary lives, away from other natives, practising their elemental craft. You thank the Elf for his information and walk back to the others, raising your arms to silence them. You explain about the Gonchong and tell them that you are going to find the Shaman alone; it would be impossible to track him down in a group. You tell them to make their own way to the fort and that you will meet them there to lead the attack in one or two days' time. They reluctantly agree to the plan and you set off immediately to find the Shaman (turn to 363).

The spear finds its target, plunging deeply into the soft green flesh of the huge Slime Sucker. Although weakened by its wound, the Slime Sucker still manages to lunge forward in attack.

SLIME SUCKER   SKILL 8   STAMINA 5

If you win, turn to 122.

203

The Lizard King finally turns to look at you, staring in disbelief at the sight of his dead pet. He steps towards you angrily, cleaving the air with his fire sword. If you are carrying a monkey on your shoulder, turn to **314**. If you are without a monkey, turn to **36**.

204

Standing precariously on the rocking raft, you draw your sword to attack the vicious Crocodile.

CROCODILE   SKILL 6   STAMINA 7

If you win, turn to **31**.

205

Your sudden movement scares the girl, and she lets go of the rope holding the Tiger. It is on top of you in one leap and you lose the first Attack Round. If you are still alive, you manage to draw your sword to defend yourself.

SABRE-TOOTHED
TIGER   SKILL 11   STAMINA 8

If you win, turn to **343**.

206

He grabs the hand-axe from you, looking very excited. The others gather round him and start to chant. They seem jubilant with their new acquisition which they seem to regard as a religious artefact. Will you:

Leave them and disappear west
into the undergrowth?   Turn to 7
Ask them for something in return?   Turn to 86
Attack them with your sword?   Turn to 359

207

The Grannit suddenly releases its grip on your shin and drops to the ground. You give it a hefty kick and watch it roll down the tunnel. The residual Rattlesnake poison in your system has killed it. The other Grannits sense what has happened and retreat into the shadowy recesses of the tunnel wall. If you possess a Pouch of Unlimited Contents, turn to 371. If you do not have this pouch, turn to 192.

208

He looks at you mistrustfully, telling you that you should have spotted his warning sign by the water pool. Nevertheless, he offers you the chance to redeem yourself and establish friendship by giving him something from your backpack in exchange for a feather from his hair. You have no choice but to comply with the request of the Shaman (make the necessary deduction on your *Adventure Sheet*). With your feather in place, the Shaman is now ready to listen to you (turn to 199).

209

You miss! The spear falls harmlessly into the water beyond the Hydra and now you must fight it with your sword.

	SKILL	STAMINA
HYDRA (left head)	9	9
HYDRA (right head)	9	9

Both heads will make a separate attack on you in each Attack Round, but you must choose which of the two you will fight each time. Attack your chosen head as in a normal battle. Against the other you will throw for your Attack Strength in the normal way, but you will not wound it if your Attack Strength is greater; you must just count this as though you have defended yourself against its bite. Of course, if its Attack Strength is greater, it will wound you. If you win, turn to 389.

210

A large boulder lands heavily on the shoulder of your sword arm. Lose 4 STAMINA points and 2 SKILL points. If you are still alive, you shield your head with your good arm and flee down the gorge as fast as you can (turn to 253).

211

You are about half-way across the beach when suddenly a large mound of sand by the sea's edge starts to rise into the air. Then you see six large spiny legs and a pair of pincers, and as the sand slides off its huge shell, your eyes widen at the daunting sight of the GIANT CRAB before you. It scuttles across the sand, picking up Mungo with one of its pincers; Mungo cries out in pain, unable to free himself from the vice-like grip. If you wish to help Mungo, turn to **182**. If you would rather run to the stone hut, turn to **307**.

212

It is soon hot and you are a little concerned that your water bottle is nearly empty. You search for water and eventually find a shallow pool of rain water in a rock basin. You drink your fill and top up your water bottle. You are about to set off again when you notice some chalk marks on the rocks by the pool. If you wish to read them, turn to **72**. If you would rather set off immediately, turn to **30**.

213

You soon arrive at yet another junction. If you wish to turn left, turn to **68**. If you wish to turn right, turn to **383**.

The Shaman is satisfied that you have earned the right to learn his secrets. He rolls his eyes up into his head and stands perfectly still with his arms outstretched. In a trance, he begins to describe the parasitic Gonchong. Its appearance is like a giant harvest spider, only its proboscis connects into the brain of its host; in this case the Lizard King. To kill it, the proboscis must be severed within seconds of its host being killed, otherwise it might leap on to its assailant in a desperate attempt to find a new host. But while it controls him, the Lizard King remains almost invincible, unharmed by normal weapons. Only fire swords can injure the host of a Gonchong. The Lizard King uses them himself, but his collection has an illusion spell cast on them to make them appear as rusty old knives that no one would steal. Using a fire sword and controlled by the Gonchong, the Lizard King is a deadly fighter. Only one creature can scare him – a monkey! Lizard Men suffer from an innate fear of monkeys, even if controlled by a Gonchong. The Shaman slowly comes out of his trance and points to the south-east, saying that the prison colony lies in that direction. You bid him farewell and walk down the side of the volcano towards the Lizard King's stronghold (turn to **168**).

215

Grabbing one of the burning brushes, you dash behind one of the huts and set it alight. Then you run to the next hut and set it on fire as well. The huts are soon blazing away, and you watch from behind the next hut as the Headhunters run around the clearing, shouting instructions to each other in total confusion. The man tied to the post is temporarily left unguarded, and you run to him to set him free. With one swipe of your sword, you cut through the vines holding him to the post, and run off towards the jungle, yelling at the man to follow. As you are running, one of the Headhunters sees you and throws his spear at you. Roll one die. If the number rolled is 1 or 2, turn to **76**. If the number rolled is 3 or 4, turn to **250**. If the number rolled is 5 or 6, turn to **323**.

216

You tell the Dwarf that you are leading the attack on the fort and ask where the Lizard King is hiding. He tells you that the Lizard King is on the fort's front battlement, urging on his troops. You tell the Dwarf that you will deal with the Lizard King and come back to free him later. You say farewell and run through the open doorway ahead (turn to **180**).

217

The Spit Toad's teeth sink painfully into your arm, but fortunately not your sword-arm. Lose 2 STAMINA points. You manage to force the Spit Toad's mouth open with your sword and roll out from under its massive belly. You stand up and lunge at it blindly.

SPIT TOAD   SKILL 5   STAMINA 6

During each Attack Round you must reduce your Attack Strength by 3 because of your blindness. If you win, turn to **134**.

218

Your legs brush against a thorny bush, instantly drawing blood. Have you drunk the aniseed-tasting liquid from the jug in the hut on the beach? If you have, turn to **258**. If you have not drunk this liquid, turn to **146**.

219

The spear flies past the pig to land harmlessly on the grass. You watch disheartened as your potential roast dinner disappears into the distance. You pick up your spear and continue west (turn to **170**).

220

The Shaman points at a boulder and ask you to lift it. You wrap your arms around it as far as you can and heave. Roll two dice. If the total is the same or less than your STAMINA score, turn to **98**. If the total is higher than your STAMINA score, turn to **369**.

221

Close to where the Giant Dragonfly now lies in a crumpled heap, you see a patch of clam-shaped fungus attached to a rotting log. If you wish to eat some of the fungus, turn to **385**. If you would rather set off again through the undergrowth, turn to **224**.

222

To your left you see movement; a small creature is running across the plain. As it approaches, you see that it is a small pig. The thought of roast suckling pig makes your mouth water. If you have a spear, turn to **342**. If you do not have a spear, turn to **167**.

223

What you see inside the chamber fills you with rage. Six Dwarfs stripped to the waist and chained together like animals are toiling with hammers at a rock face. An armoured LIZARD MAN urges them to work faster, occasionally lashing one of them across the back with its bullwhip. You put the pail down and run forward to attack the Lizard Man.

LIZARD MAN   SKILL 8   STAMINA 7

If you are still alive after two Attack Rounds, turn to **3**.

224

You decide that you have gone far enough north-west to avoid the Headhunters' village and begin to cut your way directly west through the jungle. You have not gone far when you are surprised to enter a small clearing, completely free of vegetation. A large green crystal lies in the centre of the clearing, glowing and radiating heat. Will you:

Walk round the crystal and continue west?	Turn to **71**
Touch the crystal?	Turn to **232**
Try to chip a piece off the crystal with your sword?	Turn to **370**

225

The Shaman's eyes narrow as he utters a single word – 'Liar!' Suddenly the ground begins to quake and then a huge crack opens up beneath your feet.

Steam rises out of it, scalding your leg badly. Lose 3 STAMINA points. You apologize to the Shaman for lying to him, explaining that you were only trying to gain his acceptance. You did not realize that a feather was the Shaman's symbol of peace. He grunts and touches your legs with his pole and the pain immediately disappears. Turn to **301**.

226

The tunnel narrows and you have to stoop because of the low ceiling. You appear to be in a disused part of the mine. If you wish to carry on walking down this tunnel, turn to **213**. If you would rather walk back to the last junction and turn left, turn to **101**.

227

If you possess three iron keys, turn to **273**. If you do not have any keys, turn to **162**.

228

There are several large rocks jutting out of the water which you have to steer around. It is hard work and you grow tired. You decide to pull into the bank for a while to rest. Under the shade of some trees you lie down and fall asleep. When you wake up you see that you are covered with huge mosquito bites. *Test your Luck*. If you are Lucky, turn to **236**. If you are Unlucky, turn to **103**.

229

As you hack your way through the thick under-growth you hear the distant sound of drums coming from where you saw the smoke rising. If you wish to head south-west towards it, turn to **337**. If you prefer to keep heading west, turn to **113**.

230

The force of the water crashing down on top of you is so powerful that you are almost knocked off your raft. Fortunately, you manage to stand firm, holding the pouch open. Water disappears inside it and more is drawn into it as though it is a huge blob of jelly. As quickly as it started, the turbulence dies down and the whirlpool disappears; you have caught the Water Elemental in your incredible pouch. Add 2 LUCK points. Unfortunately, your raft is breaking up and so you decide to wade over to the right-hand bank. You cannot risk releasing the Water Elemental, so you dig a hole and bury your Pouch of Unlimited Contents (make the necessary deduction on your *Adventure Sheet*). You have no option now but to continue your journey on foot (turn to 197).

231

The barrel is full of pineapples, all rotten and covered with fruit flies. But hidden behind the barrel you see a water bottle lying on the floor. You pull out the cork and sniff the contents; it might be water but there is a musty smell rising out of the bottle. If you wish to drink the liquid, turn to 6. If you would rather walk over to the door in the far wall, turn to 353.

232

Slowly and nervously you touch the glowing crystal. A warm glow radiates through your body and you feel invigorated. Add 3 STAMINA points for having benefited from the effects of the regeneration crystal. If you have not done so already, you may try to chip a piece off the crystal with your sword (turn to 370). Alternatively, you may leave the clearing and continue west through the undergrowth (turn to 71).

233

A line of rocks suddenly turns red, leading up the side of the volcano. You decide to follow the trail of the red rocks (turn to 249).

234

You struggle against the raging torrent but are unable to escape from the whirlpool made by the Water Elemental. You become weaker and weaker until you can swim no longer. You black out and are engulfed by the Water Elemental to share its watery world for ever.

235

After a short while the Marsh Hopper turns west again and you wonder whether it is tiring you out to lead you into a trap, or whether it is picking the safest path through the marsh. Your thoughts are soon answered, as a massive beast rises out of the mire in front of you. It is a two-headed HYDRA which slithers towards you on its giant slug-like body, both of its heads stretching forward to bite you. If you have a spear, turn to **272**. If you do not have a spear, turn to **29**.

236

Although the itching is almost unbearable, there are no tell-tale signs of fever. You jump back on your raft and head up-river once again (turn to **379**).

237

The Shaman shrugs his shoulders and tells you to leave immediately. He points south-east, saying that the prison colony lies in that direction. You turn around and walk down the side of the volcano towards the Lizard King's stronghold (turn to **168**).

238

The liquid tastes of aniseed and is milky in colour. You gulp it down but feel no effects and can only presume that it will protect you on the journey ahead. You put down the jug and leave the hut (turn to **152**).

239

You only manage to stop one of the quick-moving Grannits and must fight the remaining two one at a time.

	SKILL	STAMINA
First GRANNIT	4	3
Second GRANNIT	3	2

If you win, turn to **192**.

240

The pike pierces your shoulder, knocking you to the ground. Lose 2 STAMINA points and 1 SKILL point. The Hobgoblin surprisingly runs away panic-stricken rather than finishing you off. When you are well enough to walk, you stand up and cross over the archway to the other side of the ravine (turn to **139**).

241

Both the Lizard Men are standing with their backs to you as you run at them. You are able to hit one of them on the back of the head with the hilt of your sword to knock it unconscious, but you must fight the other.

LIZARD MAN   SKILL 9   STAMINA 8

If you win, turn to **189**.

242

The girl stands motionless as you run away from her. *Test your Luck*. If you are Lucky, turn to **142**. If you are Unlucky, turn to **205**.

243

One of the Pygmies steps forward and snatches the hand-axe away from you. The others gather round him and start to chant. They seem very pleased with their acquisition which they seem to regard as a religious artefact. Will you:

Leave them and disappear west
into the undergrowth? **Turn to 7**
Ask them for something in return? **Turn to 86**
Attack them with your sword? **Turn to 359**

244

You thrust your sword at the leaping Gonchong, skewering it through its bulbous abdomen. Both the Lizard King and the Gonchong are slain (turn to 400).

245

A small boulder lands on your shoulder but it strikes only a glancing blow. Lose 2 STAMINA points. You shield your head with your arms and flee down the gorge as fast as you can (turn to 253).

246

Apart from jumping, there is no way down the vertical shaft. You decide not to risk it and turn round to walk back to the junction (turn to **135**).

247

The Bear is wearing a leather collar from which hangs a tiny brass whistle. You put the whistle in your pocket and set off in search of the Shaman (turn to **27**).

248

You duck below the jet of liquid and jump back to draw your sword. You stand ready to dodge the next jet of sticky acid being spat at you by the huge SPIT TOAD in the pool. Suddenly it leaps out of the water in an attempt to kill you with its spiked teeth.

SPIT TOAD   SKILL 5   STAMINA 6

If you win, turn to **21**.

249

The head of a man suddenly pops up from behind a boulder, his hair adorned with coloured beads and feathers. He steps warily from behind the boulder holding a feathered staff in one hand and two animal bones in the other. It is the island's medicine man – the Shaman you are seeking. Are you wearing a feather in your hair? If you are, turn to **199**. If you are not, turn to **176**.

250

The spear flies through the air and strikes the poor man you have just rescued in the middle of his back. He falls to the ground with an anguished cry, now beyond any help you can give him. As the other Headhunters realize what is happening, you run back into the jungle, the noise of their shrieking voices not far behind you (turn to **102**).

251

By the time you have found all the prisoners and released them, you will have lost 4 STAMINA points in battle. If you are still alive, you are now the leader of sixty-three dedicated followers, eager for revenge (turn to **201**).

252

The Hobgoblin's eyes light up at the sight of the gold nugget. He thrusts out his hand, eagerly awaiting your bribe. You place the nugget in his hand and cross over the archway to the other side of the ravine (turn to **139**).

253

You run down the narrow gorge, hopeful that another rockfall will not occur. The gorge once again widens out and you slow down to walking pace as your claustrophobia dies down (turn to 382).

254

The battle is going badly for you as more of your men fall under the onslaught of the Lizard King's fanatical troops. You see their leader behind the line, urging them on with howling battle cries. It is a huge CYCLOPS wearing plate mail and carrying a mighty battleaxe, and you must defeat it in order to rally your men.

CYCLOPS   SKILL 10   STAMINA 10

If you win, turn to 299.

255

You slip on some loose stones as you try to dodge the spear. It sinks into your thigh with a sickening thud. Lose 3 STAMINA points. The Cave Woman screams with delight and runs down the hill waving her club. You clench your teeth and pull the spear out of your thigh and draw your sword to defend yourself.

CAVE WOMAN   SKILL 5   STAMINA 5

During each Attack Round you must reduce your Attack Strength by 2 because of the injury to your leg. If you win, turn to 79.

256

You stretch out and your fingertips just manage to reach your sword. By now you cannot breathe and your face is crimson with the veins bulging in your neck. You desperately hack at the vine until you cut through it and roll away out of its lethal range. You cough and rub your neck and watch the hideous vine drip purple sap. Although you are lucky to have escaped the clutches of the carnivorous tree, you have not escaped injury. Lose 1 SKILL point and 2 STAMINA points. Although still weary, you decide that it is better to keep on the move (turn to 81).

257

Your plan does not work. The force of the water crashing down on you is too strong and the pouch is knocked out of your hand and swept away. The raft breaks up and above the roar of the water, you hear the gurgling laughter of the Water Elemental. You gasp for air as you are forced under the pounding water. You summon all your strength and try to swim to the bank. Roll two dice. If the total is the same or less than your SKILL score, turn to 150. If the total is higher than your SKILL score, turn to 234.

258

Although the bush has poison-tipped thorns, you come to no harm. You walk on, oblivious to the danger which has passed (turn to 291).

259

Knowing that Spit Toads never share their watery domain with others, you wade confidently into the pool and pick up the casket. Back on dry land, you prise the lid off with your sword and tip the contents on to the grass. They are a glass phial containing a coloured liquid, a velvet pouch, a pair of red leather boots, and a gold ring. Will you:

Drink the liquid in the phial?	Turn to 311
Open the pouch?	Turn to 26
Try on the boots?	Turn to 94
Put the ring on your finger?	Turn to 297

260

You try to stop the leaping Gonchong with your sword, but fail. It lands on your head and skewers its proboscis into your brain. You are now controlled by the Gonchong and can only watch helplessly as the Lizard King's army annihilates your demoralized troops. The battle is lost.

261

The remaining Headhunters think you are an invincible God-empowered warrior. They turn and flee, crying out at the top of their voices. If you wish to open the hide bag lying beside the body of one of the Headhunters, turn to **187**. If you would rather head off west again, turn to **113**.

262

The approaching Lizard Man calls out to you, asking where you are heading. You cannot hope to impersonate a Lizard Man at close range and are forced to draw your sword.

LIZARD MAN   SKILL 7   STAMINA 8

As soon as you win your first Attack Round, turn to **386**.

263

You remembered not to put your sword-arm into the stone circle and so your crippled hand is not too much of a disability. Lose 1 SKILL point. You reluctantly toss one of your own items into the circle and wait to see what happens (turn to **233**).

264

Your constitution is weak and the poison runs quickly through your system. Your arm starts to throb and you break out in a sweat. Your vision blurs and you have difficulty retaining consciousness. Lose 5 STAMINA points. If your STAMINA score is now 9 or below, turn to **124**. If it is above 9, turn to **364**.

265

The Dwarfs attack the Orcs, spurred on by their hatred. The fight is soon over, the Orcs being no match for the embittered Dwarfs. Turn to **121**.

266

The door remains firmly shut. There is nothing you can do except walk back into the courtyard and try to open the other doors leading off it (turn to **84**).

267

You pull on the handle and lift up the trapdoor. In a small compartment you see a wooden box which you lift out and place on the floor. The lid is covered with candle-wax. If you wish to open the box, turn to **354**. If you would rather leave the hut, turn to **152**.

268

The doors open into a corridor which runs to the left and right of you. Prison cells with iron-barred doors line the far wall of the corridor. Looking left, the corridor comes to a dead end and so you turn right. In the end cell by a wooden door you see a frail old man sitting on a wooden bench, his leg chained to the wall. His cell door is open but the wooden door leading out of the corridor is firmly locked. Will you:

Free the old man?   Turn to **166**

Try to open the wooden door?   Turn to **227**

269

Half-way up the side of the hill to your left you see the entrance to a cave. The rocks all around the mouth of the cave are painted in bright colours, but each one has a skull resting on top of it. If you wish to climb up to the cave, turn to **59**. If you would rather walk on towards the volcano, turn to **303**.

270

You decide to attack the Lizard Men, hoping to keep one alive so that you can get some information out of it. You slip quietly out of the cover of the trees to the corner of the hut. You peep round to see the Lizard Men still talking. Drawing your sword, you charge round the corner to gain the initiative. *Test your Luck*. If you are Lucky, turn to **241**. If you are Unlucky, turn to **43**.

271

The Lizard King suddenly halts as he catches sight of your monkey. He starts to shake, his fear of monkeys quite evident. *Test your Luck*. If you are Lucky, turn to **22**. If you are Unlucky, turn to **123**.

272

As the Hydra closes in on you, you hurl the spear at one of its heads. Roll one die. If the number rolled is 1, 2, 3 or 4, turn to **209**. If the number rolled is 5 or 6, turn to **344**.

273

One of the keys fits the lock and you push the door open (turn to **395**).

274

The tunnel continues straight ahead until you arrive at the edge of a vertical downward shaft. A wooden ladder is secured to the side of it, but you cannot see down to the bottom. If you wish to climb down the ladder, turn to **315**. If you would rather return to the junction and walk past it to the other end of the tunnel, turn to **28**.

275

As soon as you touch the handle of one of the knives, it changes in appearance. Instead of a dull old knife, you find yourself holding a magnificent sword with a flaming blade; it is one of the Lizard King's own fire swords. Add 2 SKILL points and 2 LUCK points. Cutting your new weapon through the air, you make your way over to the door in the far wall (turn to 312).

276

The Pygmies grunt and shout at you, but you do not understand their language. They obviously want something from you, but you are not sure what. What do you have that you wish to give them?

A hand-axe?	Turn to 243
An iron bar?	Turn to 327
Provisions?	Turn to 126
None of these?	Turn to 137

277

It is your sword-arm which is damaged. Lose 3 SKILL points. You reluctantly toss one of your own items into the stone circle and wait to see what happens (turn to 233).

278

The tunnel comes to a dead end quite suddenly and you begin to worry that you may get lost. Lose 1 LUCK point. You turn around and walk back to the previous junction. If you wish to continue straight on, turn to 70. If you wish to turn right, turn to 172.

279

Once on the valley floor, you make your way over to a copse of trees. As soon as you enter the copse, familiar faces suddenly appear from behind the trees. The Dwarfs, Elves and men that you rescued from the mines are waiting here for your arrival. Pleased to see them again, you tell them of what has happened since you saw them last. You tell them that the fort should be attacked immediately and that you will deal with the Lizard King. You call them all together and lead them out of the copse into the valley. As you run towards the stone fort, you see its wooden gates open. The Lizard King is sending a battalion of guards and mutants out to fight you. Your small army has soon locked swords with the Lizard King's soldiers. Roll one die. If you roll 1 or 2, turn to **185**. If you roll 3 or 4, turn to **308**. If you roll 5 or 6, turn to **42**.

280

After checking yourself carefully to make sure you are finally rid of the parasites from the marsh, you continue west across the muddy plain. Ahead you see two hills and you decide to walk towards the gorge dividing them (turn to **362**).

281

Gathering momentum, you cannot stop yourself from rolling over and over into the gorge below. You land heavily with a sickening thump. Lose 2 STAMINA points. You stand up, dust yourself off, and decide to walk down the gorge (turn to **119**).

282

You open the sack carefully, in case it contains a poisonous snake. But you are surprised and pleased to see food inside: honeycomb, wheatcakes and fruit. If you wish to eat the food, turn to **116**. If you would rather save it for later and set off again, turn to **27**.

283

The ordeal is too much for you to bear, and you signal the Shaman to stop it. You have failed the test and the Shaman will not now divulge his secrets. He points south-east, saying that the prison colony lies in that direction and that you must face the Gonchong without his help. You turn around and walk down the side of the volcano towards the Lizard King's stronghold (turn to **168**).

284

You draw back from the wounded Lizard Man, offering it the chance to surrender. It throws down its sword and whip and slumps on to the ground, panting heavily. You tie its arms together behind its back with its own whip and drag it into the hut. You demand information about the slave mines, and it tells you that the entrance is not far away; about a hundred metres beyond the huts. You tie the Lizard

Man to a post and leave the hut to find the mines (turn to **147**).

285
The Goblin wakes up with a start. He reaches up and tries to grab you around the throat with his scrawny hands. If you are wearing Sog's helmet, he will not succeed, but you will have to fight him (turn to **322**). If you are not wearing a helmet, the Goblin's sharp fingernails will dig into your throat. Lose 1 STAMINA point and fight the Goblin (turn to **322**).

286
You have climbed about half-way up the vine when you see a head pop out over the edge of the platform. It belongs to an old man with grey hair who glares down at you, looking very angry. 'Go away,' he cries, 'or you'll be sorry.' If you wish to continue climbing up the vine, turn to **117**. If you wish to take his advice and slide down the vine to continue north-west, turn to **375**.

287
The Hobgoblin takes a long time to decide that you have said the wrong password. Finally it sinks in and he charges at you with his pike (turn to **328**).

288
You start to search amongst the bushes for the hidden raft and before long you find it. You drag it into the river and climb aboard. The river is not deep and you are able to push the raft up-river against the

light current quite easily with the long pole you
have (turn to 387).

289

You jump behind the hideous mutant and plunge
your sword into its back. *Test your Luck*. If you are
Lucky, turn to 144. If you are Unlucky, turn to 45.

290

The irritation becomes almost unbearable and you
cannot help but scratch at the lumps on your face.
Lose 1 STAMINA point and 1 LUCK point. If you wish
to rub your face with leaves from a nearby plant,
turn to 143. If you wish to chance eating the fungus,
turn to 110.

291

Lying dead face-down in the scrub is a seaman,
perhaps one of the crew of a pirate ship killed by the
mutant Lizard Man. A monkey strains to escape
from a chain held by the dead man's hand. If you
wish to take the monkey with you, turn to 330. If
you would rather just let it go and carry on walking,
turn to 350.

292

The helmet is over one hundred years old and once
belonged to a fabled warrior named Sog, who also
practised sorcery. Wearing the helmet will cause
any adversary to fear you so much that you will be
able to win the first Attack Round of any battle. The
adversary will only raise sufficient courage to fight

back during the second Attack Round. Wearing your new armour with pride, you walk carefully down the hill into the gorge to continue west (turn to 119).

293

By the time you have found all the prisoners and released them, you will have lost 2 STAMINA points in battle. If you are still alive, you are now the leader of sixty-three dedicated followers, eager for revenge (turn to 201).

294

The unknown power of the ring flashes a warning through your mind, telling you that the old man is an illusion projected by a fearsome Shape Changer. You dash out of the cell and slam the door shut just as the beast starts to metamorphose. Green spikes burst through its clothing and its slavering jaws open to reveal rows of razor-sharp teeth. The Shape Changer is trapped in the prison cell and you can now try to open the wooden door (turn to 227).

295

The Pygmy is insulted that you have refused his gift. He stamps on the ground and throws down his blowpipe. The other Pygmies quickly form a circle around the two of you; honour can only be restored by a duel to the death. You raise your sword to defend yourself against the enraged Pygmy.

PYGMY   SKILL 6   STAMINA 5

If you win, turn to 96.

296

The Lizard King suddenly halts as he catches sight of your monkey. He starts to shake, his fear of monkeys quite evident. He is so terrified that he can hardly raise his sword to defend himself as you rush forward. Only the mental urging of the Gonchong forces the Lizard King into token resistance.

LIZARD KING   SKILL 6   STAMINA 15

If you win, turn to 153.

297

The instant you put the ring on your finger, you feel very dizzy. You try to pull the ring off, but it will not move. The ring is cursed with a Confusion Spell. Lose 2 SKILL points. If you have not done so already, you may:

Drink the liquid in the phial	Turn to 311
Open the pouch	Turn to 26
Try on the boots	Turn to 94

If you do not wish to do any of these things, you may continue your way west across the grassy plain (turn to 222).

298

It is pitch-black inside the bore-hole, which seems to go on for miles. You decide that it is leading nowhere. There is not much room to turn round and you have to tuck your head between your legs and flip over. You scramble back down the bore-hole and are relieved to reach the main tunnel. However, when you flipped over in the bore-hole, something fell out of your backpack. Deduct one item from your Equipment List and lose 1 LUCK point. You clamber out of the bore-hole and turn right down the tunnel (turn to 47).

299

Your men are encouraged by the death of the Cyclops and push forward with new heart. As the Lizard King's troops start to fall back, you break through their line and run to the wooden gates of the fort. You enter the inner courtyard and see two sets of doors leading into the building. If you wish to walk through the double doors to your left, turn to 268. If you would rather try the doors straight ahead, turn to 84.

300

The Water Elemental crashes down on top of you, smashing the raft to pieces. Above the roar of the water you can hear the gurgling laughter of the Water Elemental. You gasp for air as you are forced under the pounding water. You summon all your strength and try to swim to the bank. Roll two dice. If the total is the same or less than your SKILL score, turn to **150**. If the total is higher than your SKILL score, turn to **234**.

301

Although the Shaman has difficulty in speaking your language, he seems to understand perfectly everything you say to him. However, before he will listen to your request for help, he insists that you wear a feather in your hair. He offers you one from his own hair, asking for something in exchange for it. You have no choice but to comply with his request (make the necessary deduction on your *Adventure Sheet*). He smiles at last, and is ready to listen to you (turn to **199**).

302

Just as you are about to take the branch, a small dog runs up to you and starts to bark. The Headhunters whirl round and shriek excitedly on seeing you. They wave their spears and clubs in the air and run towards you. If you wish to fight them, turn to **331**. If you wish to run back into the jungle, turn to **102**.

303

You eventually reach the foot of the volcano, but still see no sign of the Shaman. You look up and see the gigantic black mountain reaching up towards the sky and wonder when next it might erupt into life, belching out clouds of ash and streams of red-hot lava. You banish the thought from your mind and decide which way to head. If you wish to climb straight up the side of the volcano, turn to **178**. If

you wish to walk around the foot of the volcano, turn to 355.

304

Sharp teeth bury themselves in your neck as the sleek Razorjaw frantically tries to kill you. Lose 2 STAMINA points. If you are still alive, you try to cut the hideous creature from your neck with your sword.

RAZORJAW   SKILL 6   STAMINA 5

If you win, turn to 20.

305

Cutting down the trees with your sword is slow and tiring work. You begin to worry that the noise of the wood being cut might attract a predator, and your fears are soon realized. Standing between two trees behind you is an OGRE. He was sleeping and you have woken him. He grunts and advances towards you holding a large branch as a weapon.

OGRE   SKILL 8   STAMINA 8

If you win, turn to 99.

306

When your hand passes into the circle, you feel a pain as though it was being crushed under a cart-wheel. You withdraw it, but it is all disfigured and bent. Roll one die. If you roll 1–5, turn to 277. If you roll 6, turn to 263.

307

In your desperate attempt to flee from the Giant Crab you do not pay much attention to the sand you are running across. Suddenly, your feet land in soft, wet sand and you quickly start to sink in. You are stuck in quicksand and as you struggle you sink in faster. You scream in terror as the sand reaches your neck and the last sight you see is poor Mungo being devoured by the Giant Crab.

308

With your sword raised high, you lunge at your nearest foe. It is a LIZARD MAN.

`LIZARD MAN`   SKILL 8   STAMINA 7

If you win, turn to **341**.

309

Both the Lizard Men are standing with their backs to you as you run at them. You are able to slay one before they realize they are being attacked, but you must fight the other.

LIZARD MAN   SKILL 9   STAMINA 8

If you win, turn to **368**.

310

You fall against one of the roof-supporting beams. It is rotten and breaks under your weight. The roof caves in on top of you. You nearly asphyxiate under the debris, and are almost buried alive. Lose 4 STAMINA points. If you survive the cave-in, you manage to wriggle out of the sand and stones but are forced to return to the last junction (turn to 378).

311

You have swallowed a Potion of Clumsiness. At the beginning of any future combat, there is a possibility that you might drop your sword as you unsheathe it. Before you start the first Attack Round, roll one die. If you roll 1, you will drop your sword and automatically lose the first Attack Round. If you have not done so already, you may:

Open the pouch	Turn to 26
Try on the boots	Turn to 94
Put the ring on your finger	Turn to 297

If you do not wish to carry out any of these actions, you may continue your way west again across the grassy plain (turn to 222).

312

The door opens into a small storeroom stacked with barrels and sacks. If you wish to look inside one of the barrels, turn to **231**. If you would rather make your way over to the next door in the far wall, turn to **353**.

313

Unfortunately for you, the Headhunter at the rear of the group decides to investigate the log in which you are hiding. He pokes his head into the end of the log and calls out gleefully to the rest of the hunting party. You are trapped and your head will soon be added to their collection.

314

Are you holding a fire sword as your weapon? If you are, turn to **296**. If you are going to fight the Lizard King with an ordinary sword, turn to **271**.

315

Stepping carefully down the ladder, you eventually reach the bottom of the shaft. In the dim light you see a new tunnel, from which you hear the faint sound of singing. As you walk down the tunnel, the singing grows louder and you also hear the sound of stone being hammered. Suddenly you hear footsteps behind you. Will you:

Hide in the shadows?	Turn to 78
Turn to face whoever is approaching?	Turn to 347

316

The malaria grips your body and you become racked with fever. Lose another 3 STAMINA points and 1 SKILL point. You lose track of time as you sink into a delirious nightmare. When you finally recover from the disease, you have no idea how long you have been ill. You check your backpack and find that all your Provisions are gone, perhaps eaten by ants or maggots. You wash yourself in the river and climb on board your raft to continue your quest (turn to 379).

317

The creature halts suddenly and looks over its shoulder to stare at you in bewilderment. Its wide mouth opens and a pink forked tongue darts out and recoils just as quickly. Its big eyes look full of sorrow, but then you realize that the creature is a cunning MARSH HOPPER. Despite. their pathetic appearance, Marsh Hoppers will often lead unwary victims into the lairs of carnivorous marsh beasts for the price of a few scraps of meat. However, no creature knows how to cross treacherous marshlands better than a Marsh Hopper. The Marsh Hopper beckons you with its head to follow it across the marsh. If you wish to follow it, turn to 58. If you wish to continue west alone, turn to 158.

318

As you reach the old man, he starts to metamorphose before your eyes. Green spikes burst through his clothing and his mouth becomes a pair of slavering jaws lined with razor-sharp teeth. He is not a man but a SHAPE CHANGER, and you must fight him.

SHAPE CHANGER   SKILL 10   STAMINA 10

If you win, turn to 372.

319

The Lizard Man turns round to see who is behind it and catches sight of you sprawled on the floor. It puts down its pail and runs towards you, sword in hand. You jump up and grab your sword to fight it.

LIZARD MAN   SKILL 7   STAMINA 7

If you win, turn to 23.

320

You take careful aim and release the dagger. Unfortunately, it flies just over the top of the orange. You have failed the test and the Shaman will not now divulge his secrets. He points south-east, saying that the prison colony lies in that direction and that you must face the Gonchong without his help. You turn around and walk down the side of the volcano towards the Lizard King's stronghold (turn to 168).

321

The tunnel comes to an end at a junction. If you wish to turn left, turn to 19. If you wish to turn right, turn to 39.

322

The Goblin is a tough fighter, using anything that comes to hand to strike at you.

GOBLIN   SKILL 5   STAMINA 6

If you win, turn to 367.

323

The spear flies through the air but misses both of you. You run on as fast as you can into the jungle to escape the Headhunters. You crash through the undergrowth, oblivious to the sharp branches and thorns cutting into you. Finally, totally exhausted, you stop and lean against a tree, panting heavily. The man you have rescued is too exhausted to speak but smiles at you in gratitude. When he at last gets his breath back, he tells you that his name is Sama and he escaped from the gold mines of the Lizard King, hoping to build a raft and sail to the mainland. You tell him of your mission and he advises you to turn back, as the Lizard King is said to be invulnerable. You tell Sama that you do not fear the Lizard King and are determined to kill him. Sama replies that although he is eternally in debt to you for saving his life, he cannot face meeting the Lizard King again. You tell him that he is under no obligation and that you will fulfil your mission alone. Before shaking your hand to say goodbye, Sama hands you a bone charm which he was wearing round his neck on a leather cord. 'It will bring you good fortune,' he says calmly. Your LUCK score will now never fall below 7. Then he disappears into the undergrowth and once again you are left alone to continue your quest (turn to 113).

324

You tell the Shaman that you are not his enemy but that you have come to him for help. He stares at you coldly and says, 'Why you no wear feather if you are

friend?' If you wish to tell him that you have lost it, turn to **225**. If you wish to tell him that you did not know that it was important, turn to **208**.

325

The ground underfoot becomes rockier and the footprint trail you have been following disappears. In the distance you hear a faint rumbling – could it be the yawning of an awakening volcano? You hurry on down the gorge, but are stopped in your tracks by the sight of a huge reptile blocking your path. You stare incredulously at the armoured beast which appears some six metres in length. It is a GIANT LIZARD, and it sees you as a source of food. You must fight it.

GIANT LIZARD   SKILL 8   STAMINA 9

If you win, turn to **196**.

326

You point at the first shell. The Shaman lifts it but there is nothing underneath it. You have failed the test and he will not now divulge his secrets. He points south-east, saying that the prison colony lies in that direction and that you must face the Gon-chong without his help. You turn around and walk down the side of the volcano towards the Lizard King's stronghold (turn to **168**).

327

One of the Pygmies steps forward and snatches the iron bar away from you. He sniffs it and licks it, but does not seem very pleased with it. He gestures for you to give him something else. Will you give him:

A hand-axe?	Turn to **206**
Provisions?	Turn to **126**
Neither of these?	Turn to **137**

328

You quickly draw your sword and leap at the HOB-GOBLIN.

HOBGOBLIN   SKILL 6   STAMINA 6

If you win, turn to **338**.

329

You slip quietly out of the cover of the trees to the corner of the hut. You peep round to see the Lizard Men still talking. Drawing your sword, you charge round the corner to gain the initiative. *Test your Luck*. If you are Lucky, turn to **309**. If you are Unlucky, turn to **163**.

330

The monkey happily sits on your shoulder and you set off again in the company of your new friend (turn to **350**).

331

Despite your great fighting ability, there are just too many Headhunters for you to overcome. You manage to slay four of them before a spear is thrust into your back to end your quest.

332

The powder is not only decorative, but also magical. It belonged to a wizard who was press-ganged into slavery by the Lizard Men. However, before he went into the mines, the wizard discarded the bottle containing the powder, hoping that somebody might find it. It was discovered by the Cave Woman who did nothing with it except empty it into her clay bowl. The powder will protect you from any person or being who tries to control your mind. Add 2 LUCK points. There is nothing else of interest in the cave, so you decide to leave (turn to 17).

333

As you lift the breastplate off the nail, it scrapes against the wall. *Test your Luck*. If you are Lucky, turn to 164. If you are Unlucky, turn to 285.

334

You stretch out your arm and manage to grab a bush to stop yourself rolling down the hill. Lying on the ground you see a hollow under a rock, but it is too dark to see inside. If you wish to reach into the hollow, turn to 145. If you would rather walk carefully down into the gorge to continue west, turn to 119.

335

The Shaman hands you a dagger and tells you to throw it at an orange which he places on the top of a rock. Roll two dice. If the total is the same or less than your SKILL score, turn to 93. If the total is higher than your SKILL score, turn to 320.

336

A large boulder lands heavily on your shoulder, fortunately not that of your sword-arm. Lose 3 STAMINA points and 1 SKILL point. If you are still alive, you shield your head with your good arm and flee down the gorge as fast as you can (turn to 253).

337

The beating of the drums grows louder as you scramble through the undergrowth towards them. You also hear chanting voices and deep humming. You crawl forward as quietly as you can until you reach the edge of a small clearing. There are several bamboo huts in a circle around the edge of the clearing. In the centre of the clearing you see twelve Headhunters standing around a half-naked man tied to a post. One of the Headhunters, who is wearing a face-mask and head-dress, steps forward, his arms raised in the air. The drums instantly stop beating. Then a woman hands him a bone knife – the Headhunters are about to gain a new trophy. There are too many of them for you to fight at once, and you feel helpless. There is only one plan you can think of to distract the Headhunters, but it is dangerous. If you wish to take a burning branch from the fire in front of you and set some of the huts on fire, turn to 171. If you would rather slip back into the jungle and continue west, turn to 113.

338

There is a leather pouch hanging from the Hobgoblin's belt. If you want to open it, turn to 374. If you would rather hurry across the ravine, turn to 139.

339

The Spit Toad leaps at you at the same instant that you thrust your sword out in front of you. The weight of the Spit Toad knocks you to the ground but your sword has found its mark; the blade is lodged up to the hilt in the Spit Toad's throat. It shudders in its death throes, while you crawl out from under its massive belly. Gradually your vision returns and you retrieve your sword. If you still wish to drink at the pond, turn to 92. If you would rather head off west again, turn to 222.

340

You draw your swords and run down on to the beach hoping to catch the Pirates off guard. You manage to cut two down before they are able to draw their cutlasses and then you each fight two of the remaining four at the same time.

	SKILL	STAMINA
First PIRATE	7	7
Second PIRATE	8	6

Both Pirates will make a separate attack on you in each Attack Round, but you must choose which of the two you will fight. Attack your chosen Pirate as in a normal battle. Against the other you will throw for your Attack Strength in the normal way, but you will not wound him if your Attack Strength is greater; you must just count this as though you have defended yourself against his blow. Of course, if his Attack Strength is greater, he will wound you. If you defeat them both, turn to **61**.

341

You look round to see how the battle is going. Many of your fellow fighters are slain and the rest are in retreat. If you have the Horn of Valhalla, turn to **109**. If you do not have this horn, turn to **254**.

342

The pig is running very swiftly and you have to throw fast. *Test your Luck*. If you are Lucky, turn to **115**. If you are Unlucky, turn to **219**.

343

The girl starts to cry and you are suddenly filled with remorse for having killed her Tiger. You think about consoling her, but she runs away up the hill as fast as a gazelle. Lose 2 LUCK points. You sheathe your sword and descend into the valley to reconnoitre with the freed slaves (turn to **279**).

344

A perfect throw! The spear flies up into the open jaw of one of the Hydra's heads and reappears at the back. The head slumps forward completely lifeless, but the Hydra still attacks you with its surviving head.

HYDRA   SKILL 9   STAMINA 9

If you win, turn to 389.

345

You manage to crawl out backwards from underneath the rubble. Lying amidst all the rocks and stones is a small wooden box. You prise the lock open with your sword, and shout for joy when you see what is lying inside. It is a hunting horn, but the runes carved on it tell you it is no ordinary horn. It is the legendary Horn of Valhalla. When blown, it will fill its player and all his friends who can hear it with strength and courage. Add 2 LUCK points. You sling the horn round your neck and walk back to the last junction. If you wish to turn left, turn to 172. If you wish to head straight on, turn to 278.

346

The strength with which the Lizard King attacks you is overpowering. Blow after blow of his fire sword crashes down on you and it is all you can do to defend yourself. Your own sword is useless, unable to make even a scratch on the Lizard King. You are forced to back off and as you tire, the Lizard King finds a gap in your defence. His fire sword cuts a terrible gash into your arm, forcing you to drop your sword. He picks you up and hurls you over the battlements to the delight of his troops below. The day is lost and the Lizard King will remain ruler of Fire Island for ever.

347

Walking down the tunnel towards you is a LIZARD MAN carrying a pail. It looks surprised to see you and drops its pail to the ground. With a guttural cry it runs forward to attack you with its scimitar.

LIZARD MAN   SKILL 7   STAMINA 7

If you win, turn to 23.

348

While you are asleep, a Vampire Bat flutters down to feast on your blood. You do not feel its fangs sink into your ankle and it is only when you awake that you see the punctures in your skin. Lose 2 STAMINA points. You shudder at the sight of the wound and pack your belongings quickly before starting off again (turn to 212).

349

As you climb on to the platform, the old man throws down his pole and climbs higher up into the tree. He is very agile and you will not catch up with him carrying your sword and backpack. You decide to leave him alone and climb back down the vine to continue north-west (turn to 375).

350

Over the scrubland and one more hill, and you find yourself overlooking a green valley. A stone fortress lies in the middle of the valley, its striped flag fluttering in the breeze. At last you have found the prison colony. You are about to walk down into the valley when you hear a growl behind you. It is a huge SABRE-TOOTHED TIGER held on a rope by a blonde girl with wild feline eyes. She stares at you inquisitively as the Tiger strains on its leash. Will you:

Try to communicate with her?	Turn to **106**
Attack the Tiger with your sword?	Turn to **190**
Run away into the valley?	Turn to **242**

351

The liquid hits your face and your eyes start to sting. You have been temporarily blinded by the sticky acid of a SPIT TOAD. You realize what is happening and draw your sword. You know the Spit Toad will try to leap on you and kill you with its spiked teeth. You cut your sword blindly through the air and step back from the pond, rubbing your eyes with your free hand. Although you cannot see it, the Spit Toad suddenly leaps at you. *Test your Luck.* If you are Lucky, turn to **339**. If you are Unlucky, turn to **73**.

352

On the side of the volcano, you see a flash of light which could be sunlight reflected on a mirror or polished blade. Could it be the Shaman or one of the Lizard King's patrols? You intend to find out and hurry on (turn to **399**).

353

The door is not locked and opens into a room which is filled with benches and stools. Glass beakers, flasks and tumblers sit on top of the benches, and shelves on the wall are lined with jars containing curious compounds. You are standing in the Lizard King's laboratory. Suddenly you hear footsteps coming from the other side of a door in the far wall. If you wish to draw your sword to meet whoever is about to enter the laboratory, turn to **360**. If you would rather hide under one of the benches, turn to

77

354

The lid lifts up easily and inside you find a corked earthenware jug and a note which reads: 'Many years ago I came to Fire Island for peace and solitude. But since the Lizard Men have dwelt here, such an existence is no longer possible. I have now returned to the mainland. Many of the plants and bushes here are poisonous; a scratch can kill you. Drink my potion from this jug and you will come to no harm. I wish you well for whatever reason you are here. Farewell, Baskin.' If you wish to drink the liquid in the jug, turn to 238. If you would rather leave the hut immediately, turn to 152.

355

As you walk along, you become aware of a strong smell of sulphur in the air. You soon arrive at the edge of a giant pool of thick yellow mud with large gas bubbles breaking through its surface and making unpleasant plopping sounds. The pool must be quite hot judging by the heat radiating from it. Lying in a strange nest of stones and sticks, you see two large eggs that look like melons. Their shells are yellow and wrinkled, and you have no idea what creature might have laid them by the side of the sulphur pool to incubate. If you wish to take a closer look at the eggs, turn to 48. If you would rather climb up the volcano, turn to 178.

356

The door flies open (turn to 395).

357

The snake bite is fatal. There is nothing you can do to stop the effects of the poison, and there is nobody around to help you. Your adventure ends on a barren hill on Fire Island.

358

You point at the middle shell. The Shaman lifts it and you are relieved to see the bead lying underneath it. You have passed the test. If you have now passed three tests, turn to **214**. If not, which will you try next?

Fear	Turn to **75**
Pain	Turn to **151**
Revulsion	Turn to **183**
Strength	Turn to **220**
Dexterity	Turn to **335**

359

You do not advance more than two steps before the Pygmies raise their blowpipes to their mouths to fire six darts at you. Roll one die to determine the number of darts that stick in your flesh and deduct 1 STAMINA point for each. If you are still alive, turn to **373**.

360

The door flies open and a Dwarf shackled by his arms and legs is pushed into the laboratory by a grotesque two-headed LIZARD MAN. The mutant sees you and snarls. He hurls the poor Dwarf to one side and strides forward to attack you with his scimitar.

TWO-HEADED			
LIZARD MAN	SKILL 9		STAMINA 9

If you win, turn to **173**.

361

You arrive back at the bore-hole where the unfortunate Dwarf still lies beside his hand-cart. If you now wish to climb into the bore-hole, turn to **298**. If you would rather walk past it, turn to **47**.

362

The ground rises and you are at last away from the difficult terrain – the jungle and marsh are behind you. Grass and flowers make the island appear lush and beautiful, but you know you cannot afford to relax. It is not long before you reach the gorge and see that it runs between several hills in a westerly direction. If you wish to walk down the gorge, turn to **40**. If you would rather climb the hill to your right, turn to **194**.

363

You walk down to the river and jump on your raft. Progress against the current is slow as the river narrows and the water runs faster. If you still wish to journey by raft, turn to **228**. If you would rather walk overland, turn to **376**.

364

Although you are dangerously weak from the effects of the poison, you survive. You rest until finally you feel strong enough to continue your quest. If you now wish to drive the Rattlesnake out of its hole with your sword, turn to **5**. If you would rather walk carefully down into the gorge to head west, turn to **119**.

365

There is no other evidence of the Shaman's where-abouts and so you follow your hunch and walk on towards the volcano (turn to **269**).

366

Kneeling down beside the crushed body of Mungo, you gently lift his head in your arms. His eyes open a little and he manages half a smile despite his agony. In a whisper he says, 'Well, old friend, it's the end of the road for me. A lot of use I've been. Make sure you get the Lizard King for me, won't you?' Then his eyes close and he slumps down dead. You bury him on the beach near the cliff, marking the grave with his sword skewered into the sand. More determined than ever, you set off on your quest and walk to the stone hut (turn to **198**).

367

You take the breastplate and just manage to squeeze into it. Add 1 SKILL point. You leave the Goblin's room and walk to the spiral staircase (turn to **8**).

368

You quickly search the bodies of the Lizard Men. In one of their pockets you find three iron keys which you put in your own pocket. Not wasting any more time, you run off to find the slave mines (turn to 147).

369

The boulder is too heavy for you to lift and you are forced to give up trying. You have failed the test and the Shaman will not now divulge his secrets. He points south-east, saying that the prison colony lies in that direction and that you must face the Gonchong without his help. You turn around and walk down the side of the volcano towards the Lizard King's stronghold (turn to 168).

370

You swing your sword and bring it down heavily on to the rock. To your dismay, the blade snaps in two, leaving you with a much-shortened sword. Lose 2 SKILL points. If you have not already done so, you may touch the crystal (turn to 232). Alternatively, you may leave the clearing and continue west through the undergrowth (turn to 71).

371

You decide to put a Grannit in the pouch, hoping that it might be a useful decoy for you later. You poke around the wall and prise one away and drop it into the pouch. Walking on down the tunnel, you finally arrive at a dead end. You have no option but to turn around and walk back to the junction (turn to 57).

372

You leave the cell and its gruesome inmate and try to open the wooden door (turn to 227).

373

The darts are tipped with a tranquillizing compound. You fall unconscious to the ground, and when you wake up again the Pygmies are nowhere to be seen. Your sword is still in your hand, but your backpack is empty. You have lost all your possessions and Provisions. Lose 2 LUCK points. You curse the Pygmies and set off west again (turn to 7).

374

Inside the pouch you find a tiny clay doll. It was made by a witch doctor and is cursed. Lose 2 LUCK points. You throw the doll down the ravine and cross the archway (turn to **139**).

375

Hacking your way through plants and shrubs, you become aware of a buzzing sound above you. Hovering over you is the colourful but threatening shape of a GIANT DRAGONFLY, its iridescent wings beating fast, yet keeping the Dragonfly perfectly still. Suddenly it plunges down to attack you.

GIANT
DRAGONFLY   SKILL 8   STAMINA 4

If you win, turn to **221**.

376

You steer the raft over to the right-hand bank and jump off. The terrain all around is tree-covered hillside with plenty of rocks and bushes to make walking quite arduous. You look around and decide to set off towards the volcano in the north-west as it might be an ideal place for the Shaman to hide. After trudging your way through the undergrowth, you suddenly notice a strange-looking bush. It has wide leaves with crimson tips and fruit like giant raspberries hanging from its branches. If you wish to eat some of the fruit, turn to **100**. If you would rather keep walking, turn to **399**.

377

The paste stings mildly, but has no beneficial or detrimental effect. There is none left to try eating, so you take your sword and start to hack your way west again (turn to **113**).

378

At the junction you may either continue straight on (turn to **68**) or turn left (turn to **4**).

379

For no apparent reason, the water becomes very turbulent. A whirlpool forms in front of the raft and you have to cling on to stop yourself from being flung off. Suddenly a great wall of water rises out of the whirlpool, forming itself into a vague humanoid shape. You are about to be engulfed by a WATER ELEMENTAL. If you possess a Pouch of Unlimited Contents, turn to **181**. If you do not have this item, turn to **300**.

380

You wait about fifteen minutes before chancing leaving the safety of the log. Fortunately, the Headhunters are nowhere to be seen. You waste no time in drawing your sword to cut a new path west (turn to **113**).

381

You manage to cling on to the tree with one hand and knock the Tarantula off the trunk with your other hand. You continue your climb and cut off a bunch of bananas. Back on the ground you devour them quickly and walk back to your shelter. Add 2 STAMINA points. You crawl into your shelter to settle down for the night, wondering what events the next day will bring. Looking up, you see wispy clouds in shades of pink and purple gradually deepen in colour as the night sky takes over from the day. Despite the deafening noise of thousands of insects enjoying the cool night air, you are soon fast asleep. *Test your Luck*. If you are Lucky, turn to **388**. If you are Unlucky, turn to **348**.

382

On a large boulder to your right you see some words which seem to have been carved out of the stone. If you want to walk up to the boulder and read the words, turn to **35**. If you would rather continue your trek down the gorge, turn to **119**.

383

The tunnel is now very narrow and the beams supporting the roof are cracked and dislodged in places. You feel very claustrophobic in the dim light, but you press on, often being showered with dust and small stones. You do not see a rock on the floor and stumble over it. *Test your Luck*. If you are Lucky, turn to **140**. If you are Unlucky, turn to **310**.

384

Before the Gonchong can withdraw its proboscis from the Lizard King, you slice through it with your sword. Both the Lizard King and the Gonchong are slain (turn to **400**).

385

As you reach out to break off one of the fungi, its clam-like top opens up and releases a jet of spores into your face. They irritate your skin and lumps appear on your face. Your eyes start to close as the irritation increases. Will you:

Ignore it and hope it will go away?	Turn to **290**
Rub your face with leaves from a nearby plant?	Turn to **143**
Eat the fungus?	Turn to **110**

386

The Dwarfs run to help you and the Lizard Man is soon overpowered. You line up the Dwarfs again and set off along the tunnel (turn to **114**).

387

You have not gone far before you realize that you are not safe even aboard your raft. You see a pair of eyes protruding from the water ahead of you, and suddenly a huge jaw lined with sharp teeth gapes open. With great force, the CROCODILE slams into your raft, almost knocking you off it. The Crocodile thrashes around in the water, its jaws opening and snapping shut in its desperation to bite you. If you have an iron bar, turn to **9**. If you do not have an iron bar, turn to **204**.

388

The night passes without incident and you wake early to continue your quest (turn to **212**).

389

As the Hydra sinks down into the black mire, the Marsh Hopper takes flight, his treachery revealed. He runs off in great loping strides and is soon out of sight. There is nothing else to do except to trudge your way west. However, you have gone not more than a hundred metres when you notice turbulence in the water to your right. That infernal Marsh Hopper has led you into a section of the marsh seething with carnivorous life. Swimming quickly towards you is a GIANT WATER-SNAKE and you must fight for your life in the marshlands yet again.

GIANT WATER-
SNAKE   SKILL 6   STAMINA 5

During each Attack Round you must reduce your Attack Strength by 2 because of your tiredness and lack of mobility compared with the Snake. If you win, turn to **49**.

390

On the right bank of the river you see a man dressed in tattered clothing. He is waving his arms around frantically and calling out to you. He looks as if he could be an escaped prisoner. If you wish to steer your raft over to the man, turn to **87**. If you would rather keep pushing up-river, turn to **14**.

391

The undergrowth between the trees is dense; plants with long or broad leaves, some with spiny tips, vines, creepers, fungi, roots and flowers of all sizes, shapes and colours fighting for light and space in the humid jungle thicket. You have to use your sword to cut your way through it, and it is a long and slow business. If you wish to sit down and rest at the base of a great tree, turn to **53**. If you would rather continue hacking your way west, turn to **81**.

A thought suddenly crosses your mind that perhaps
the boots you are wearing might be enchanted. You
put your foot up against the wall and try to walk up
it. Sure enough, it works. You are wearing a magical
pair of Boots of Climbing. Add 1 LUCK point. You
climb down the wall and somewhat apprehensively
step over to the edge of the shaft. It feels very
strange to be walking vertically down the wall like a
fly. The shaft is deep but you eventually reach the
bottom. It is almost totally dark. You feel your way
along the wall but cannot find another tunnel leading off the abandoned shaft. You are about to step
back up the side of the shaft when your foot comes
into contact with something. You bend down and
feel the blade of a sword. You step back up to the
tunnel above to examine your discovery. In the
yellow light of the torches you admire the superbly
crafted sword you are holding. Add 2 SKILL points.
You throw your old sword down the shaft and walk
back to the junction (turn to 135).

393

The Dwarf's shackles are soon undone by the pick-lock's wire. Add 1 LUCK point. You tell him that you are leading the attack on the prison colony and ask where the Lizard King is hiding. He tells you that the Lizard King is on the fort's front battlement, urging on his troops. You tell the Dwarf to take the mutant's scimitar and help his fellow men outside. You wish him good luck and run through the open doorway ahead (turn to **180**).

394

Before the Slime Sucker is close enough to attack you, you throw the spear at it. Roll one die. If the number rolled is 1 or 2, turn to **191**. If the number rolled is 3, 4, 5 or 6, turn to **202**.

395

You find yourself standing in a dingy torture chamber. It is full of terrible instruments of pain: racks, thumbscrews, iron maidens and whips. You also see some rusty knives lying on a table in the corner of the chamber. Will you:

Pick up a whip?	Turn to **136**
Pick up a rusty knife?	Turn to **275**
Ignore everything and head for the door in the far wall?	Turn to **312**

396

The Spit Toad's teeth sink painfully into your sword-arm. Lose 2 STAMINA points and 2 SKILL points. You grab your sword with your other hand and manage to force open the Spit Toad's mouth with it. You roll out from under its massive belly and stand up to lunge at it blindly.

SPIT TOAD   SKILL 5   STAMINA 6

During each Attack Round you must reduce your Attack Strength by 3 because of your blindness. If you win, turn to **134**.

397

The Shaman tells you that you must pass three different tests from a choice of six and asks you which you wish to take first. Which will you try?

Luck	Turn to **2**
Fear	Turn to **75**
Pain	Turn to **151**
Revulsion	Turn to **183**
Strength	Turn to **220**
Dexterity	Turn to **335**

398

You prise open the chest and are surprised at its contents – iron bars! The captain must have tricked his crew into believing they were burying treasure and the real treasure is probably still on board his ship, not that it will do him much good now. You decide to put one of the iron bars in your backpack and walk over to the goat-track to climb the cliff (turn to **200**).

399

You notice a bulging sack hanging from the branch of a tree on the end of a piece of rope. If you wish to cut the sack down, turn to **282**. If you would rather keep walking, turn to **27**.

400

You throw the vile Gonchong over the wall and stand on the battlements in full view of your men. A cheer rises from below and you watch with satisfaction as they easily defeat the Lizard King's demoralized troops. The battle is over and victory is yours. The Elves, Dwarfs and men can now return to their homes on the mainland and the slave mines of Fire Island will close for ever. Mungo would have been proud of you.

Judy Blume

Judy Blume <u>knows</u> about growing up. She has a knack for going right to the heart of even the most secret problems and feelings. You'll always find a friend in her books—like these from Laurel-Leaf!

____ARE YOU THERE, GOD? IT'S ME, MARGARET......	90419-6-62	$2.50
____BLUBBER............................	90707-1-14	2.50
____DEENIE..............................	93259-9-69	2.50
____IT'S NOT THE END OF THE WORLD................	94140-7-29	2.50
____STARRING SALLY J. FREEDMAN AS HERSELF........................	98239-1-55	2.75
____THEN AGAIN, MAYBE I WON'T..................................	98659-1-15	2.50
____TIGER EYES........................	98469-6-23	2.50

═══ LAUREL-LEAF BOOKS ═══